W9-BII-938

FOWL
PLAY

Also by Patricia Tichenor Westfall

Real Farm

FOWL PLAY

A Molly West Mystery
PATRICIA TICHENOR WESTFALL

St. Martin's Press
New York

FOWL PLAY. Copyright © 1996 by Patricia Tichenor Westfall. Printed in the United States of America. No part of this book may be used or reproduced in any manner whatsoever without written permission except in the case of brief quotations embodied in critical articles or reviews. For information, address St. Martin's Press, 175 Fifth Avenue, New York, N.Y. 10010.

Design by Nancy Resnick

Library of Congress Cataloging-in-Publication Data

Westfall, Patricia Tichenor.
    Fowl play : a Molly West mystery / by Patricia Tichenor Westfall.
—1st ed.
        p.   cm.
    ISBN 0-312-14604-3
    I. Title.
PS3573.E865F6   1996
813'.54—dc20   96-24562
                                                  CIP

First Edition: November 1996

10   9   8   7   6   5   4   3   2   1

For my mother:
A champion listmaker

FOWL
PLAY

THURSDAY

KEN

He rustled, rattled, coughed. He rustled again, then with illogical pauses, began: "This is Wrongbutton in the morning with the news. Lead . . . story: the school bus Martha . . . Sherwin drives has been in for transmission work but is . . . fine now. Next up: Slim Coolis' . . . new Nubian goat has just had triplets, all useless billies. Hey Slim, too bad; better luck next time. Next: Sheriff Matins's checking out a murder. Next: Gloria Parri"—that's when the rightly named Wrongbutton punched a wrong button and ended his newscast.

Molly sighed. Only Wrongbutton would put a murder after goat triplets. She turned off the radio and reached to phone Matins. The sheriff lived next door, if a half mile away through the woods was indeed next door. Practically made him family. If there were a murder in the county she had a right to know. Neighbor's prerogative. But with a murder, would he be home? She reached for her robe instead of the phone. Later, she thought, call him later. After coffee.

Molly West faced her mornings slowly, reluctantly, always beginning the dour negotiation with her toes since the only decent mirror in the house was at the base of her stairs. As she came down every morning, her bare feet would appear first in the mirror; then would come the hem of her old blue robe. She'd straighten her torso as it descended into view, momentarily noting her thickened waist and arms. She'd pat her hair as it appeared, frowning automatically at the sprinkling of gray. Then she'd forget about her fifty-two-year-old reality. Molly was comfortable with middle age.

In the kitchen, her husband, Ken, was holding a puppy in one hand and shuffling some newspapers inside a training cage with the other.

"I think he got through the night. The papers are dry," he said. The puppy squirmed happily. A week ago he'd been a half-starved orphan in a cage at the pound. The Puppy Rescue Association then picked this wriggling mottlement of uncertain heritage as a "good candidate for adoption," if first he had some foster care to get him healthy. Molly and Ken were his foster—is it parents?—for a few weeks until he was ready for a home. The couple had helped found Puppy Rescue in the Tricounty and were enthusiastic supporters—too enthusiastic sometimes, because they occasionally kept the puppies. Goldie, for example, their older and, for the moment, only other dog was a Puppy Rescue dog.

"Where is Goldie?" Molly said.

"I don't know." He handed her the puppy and picked up his briefcase. This was the first week of classes for Ken—or Dr. K as the students called him—a sociology professor. He kissed her and left but shouted back through the screen, "Molly, students are coming out tonight." His Appalachian Culture class was to organize its annual community service project.

Ken, too, was comfortable with middle age, and—for the moment—with life in general. His hair was thin but not gone, his stomach broadening but not bulbous under his sport jacket, tie and jeans—the nineties uniform of the deliberately cool professor. Although he was content with his work now, eight years ago he'd begun a three-year sulk because being a sociology professor at Sycamore State, an eight-thousand-student college in the rugged emptiness of Appalachian Ohio was not the same as being a sociology professor at Harvard.

Or Princeton.

Or even plain old Ohio State.

He was a second-rate professor at a second-rate college in the middle of a second-growth woods. It was a school without graduate students, without research opportunities or, for that matter, without a sociology department. He was the lone sociologist in a "social science" department, so he didn't even have colleagues for one-upmanshipping.

It wasn't supposed to have been like this. He and Molly met at the University of Illinois–Chicago Circle when both were working on BBAs. It was the sixties, so as was customary they'd lived together about three years, then married, then had the kids, Amanda and Todd. Molly worked at a series of bookkeeping jobs before landing a position as benefits manager at a Loop bank, but Ken took a job as an accounts manager for the Chicago Housing Agency right out of college. It gave him a taste of poverty. He was galvanized and fascinated. So with Molly's support, he started working on his Ph.D. in sociology at the University of Chicago.

Unfortunately, he finished (with honors—his dissertation was on anomie in urban housing projects) just in time for the glut of Ph.D.s in the late seventies. The only place that even offered him an interview was remote Sycamore State. Molly agreed to the move because she believed, wrongly it turned out, that bookkeepers could find work anywhere.

Southern Ohio was not what either expected. Ken's image was of the occasional Holstein on the occasional hillock. Molly's image was of rusting factories and rivers that could catch fire. Instead they found rough, rugged terrain, deeply wooded, lush with plant and animal life, where Ken could contemplate rural instead of urban poverty. His regular courses at the department now included Poverty in America, Appalachian Culture, Criminal Behavior, and the ever exciting Beginning Sociology.

Yet this wasn't the fame, glory or valorous revamping of troubled society he'd planned for his career. So he had been miserable. Tenured, but miserable.

Then one morning Molly was prattling. She often chattered after coffee, so that wasn't odd. Once awake, she acted awake. But he hadn't heard a word she'd said. "What did you just say?" he interrupted.

"I said the ironweed is about to bloom again."

He sat a minute. "What is ironweed?"

Molly stared openmouthed. "We've lived here half our married lives."

"I know that. I mean, I know that flower. Don't tell me." He shrugged, embarrassed.

"It's the purple one," she said gently. "Tall. Like a carrot in bloom. Fills the fields in August."

"Ah, the weed you've tried to train into a fake shrub in the back."

"That one."

"Molly, what are we doing here?"

"Raising kids. Vegetables. Puppies. Not to mention Amanda's goat and Todd's rabbits."

"No, Molly, you know what I mean. You were going to be a bank president. I was going to be a hotshot academic."

"Vice president. Bank vice president. I never meant to be uppity."

"Vice president. Yes, of course." He sighed. "Do you know why I've been unhappy?"

Molly waited, hoping. She was tired of his constant grumpiness.

"I'm unhappy because I like it here."

"What?"

"I like it here. I love the land, the woods. I like being the only professor in a one-man department. I like chasing Amanda's stupid goat. I like the people here. I don't like how poor they are, but I like trying to change things. I like it here, but this isn't success. I've been fighting the feeling, I think, because if I admit I'm happy, I also admit I'm a nobody and will always be a nobody."

"Is it time for my mushy 'You're somebody to me' speech?"

"Have you had two cups of coffee yet?"

"No."

"Then please, no speeches."

That was five years ago, five years of grand contentment, especially for Molly, because, unlike Ken, she had fallen in love with the region within months of their arriving fifteen years ago this past summer. One of her fears those first few years was that Ken would get so dissatisfied he'd try to find a better college, one in a big town or, worse, an urban corridor. Molly had grown up in Chicago suburbs. Her idea of hell was a quiet suburban street with neat lawns. Here they lived on a messy thirty acres of woods, wildflowers, streams, brambles and fauna ranging from the slimy to the fuzzy. She loved it all.

To return to the control of towns would be to leave the only place she'd ever felt at home. She wasn't sure why she, who had been born on Chicago's Near North Side, who'd learned to walk in a Chicago park, who still talked with a Chicago twang, could feel at home here. But she did. The now routine rattle and squeaks of raccoons as they descended from trees at dusk had terrified her at first, but now she couldn't imagine life without the racket.

The people, too, had scared her in the beginning. They all had shotguns in their pickups, and she didn't know which was stranger, the guns or the pickups. Now she had her own pickup. And her own shotgun. "Molly"—Sheriff Matins had surprised her one day—"sometimes I think you're one of us."

Molly set the puppy on the grass. The puppy performed. He's housebroken, she thought gratefully. Then she saw a movement through the woods. Matins, on the now well-worn foot trail between their two houses. And behind him, wagging her tail, smiling her golden retriever (sprinkled with a possible dash of husky or collie) smile, was Goldie. Oh no, Molly thought, she's been in his chickens again.

___2

MATINS

Sheriff John Matins' friendship with Molly was comfortable and predictable, about nine-tenths mutual respect and one-tenth basic crankiness. She was sure he was coming over mainly to tell her about the murder. He would, however, pretend he didn't plan to tell her. He would also act irate about Goldie's hen-chasing expedition, but she knew just as surely from long experience with Appalachian conversation that he would start with something else, anything else, instead. It was complicated talking with natives.

But if she wanted to know the news, she'd have to try to be Appalachian indirect herself. Trouble was, for fifteen years she'd been trying. Always there'd be a slip into brashness on her part. She'd ask too direct a question or be too natural, too open in her reactions. Such behavior was not acceptable in a region where understatement was a high art form. Matins liked to provoke Molly until she spluttered in frustration, thus revealing herself again for the foreigner she was. Betty, John's wife, was always scolding him for baiting newcomers—anyone who'd lived less than fifty years in the area being a newcomer, of course.

Molly watched his slow progress toward the house and decided she had time to make her list before he arrived. This was Molly's second confrontation with waking reality, her morning to-do list. Coffee cooling at hand, she'd pull off yesterday's *Far Side* cartoon, flip it and start bulleting the day's tasks. This time Gary Larson's vision was of suburban dinosaurs saying goodbye to their visitors, the Stegosaurs, who'd left punctures in the furniture. Made her think of the students coming over tonight.

As always the first item on her list was•Make a list, so she could have something to cross off when she finished. Today the second item was•Plan and buy snacks for the students. She erased that and made it two items:•Plan the snacks.•Buy the snacks. Why get credit for one thing if she did two? The list continued:•Drive for the Meal Van—about 11:00.•Call about tuckpointing the foundation.•Help set up the Meal Van booth at the county fairgrounds. •Haircut, if time. She was trying to decide whether to put laundry on the list—or rather•Sort laundry.•Wash laundry.•Dry laundry.•Put laundry away—why get credit for one thing if she did four?—when John Matins tapped on the screen door.

"Coffee, John?"

"Nope; had enough. Had a second cup yet?" Molly's morning rhythms were known to all the neighbors.

"Just starting it." She brought her coffee and list out to the porch. Late August was warm in the early mornings, even though the light through the trees was beginning to have a fall slant. They sat down in the scarred old redwood chairs on the porch. How long would he torture her before telling her about the murder? she wondered.

"List done?" Matins said. Molly's lists were also much discussed around the county, sometimes with admiration, sometimes with hoots of laughter.

"List is done," Molly said. "Care to inspect?" I can be patient, I can be patient, she thought.

Matins picked up the list. "A fair booth?"

"Sort of an outreach program; we're trying to help senior citizens who need home meal delivery to find us."

He turned the list over to read the cartoon. "Not bad," he said, "but I like the ones where snakes wear glasses better."

"I like the ones with chickens," Molly said. Pretty subtle, she thought; that'll get him to the topic. But no . . .

"How come you never date your lists?"

"I don't need to. Yesterday's date is always on the back. See? The cartoon is Wednesday's, so this must be Thursday's list."

Matins shook his head. "That puppy housebroke yet?" That puppy had been chomping Molly's, then John's and now Goldie's feet. Goldie calmly clamped a paw on him. He squealed and yelped, she sighed and put her head down but did not let go.

"Got through the night," Molly said.

"Yeah? Well, an older dog around helps the young ones learn faster, assumin' the old dog stays home."

Ah, progress, Molly thought. Almost to the topic. Maybe. She wondered why he played this game. He always gave in eventually. He, like most hill folk, enjoyed a good story, liked it even better if he were doing the telling, so why hold out?

"I'm not sure when Goldie took off," Molly said. "Maybe this morning when Ken got up; maybe we forgot to bring her in last night."

"I see while that dog of yourn was nosing around my hens this morning she still don't have any tags," he said—very slowly, with mock sternness. This was also a long-standing routine for them. Molly didn't believe she should have to buy license tags for strays, although Goldie, now five, had first strayed into the household at about six months old.

"While my dog was nosing around your hens, Wrongbutton

said you were investigating a murder. So why were you at home to hassle my dog?" Molly retorted, secretly impressed with herself. She'd been indirect, just like a local. The murder was now in the conversation, after only five preliminary subtopics.

"Did most of that crime scene stuff last night. Besides, know who did it; nothing to investigate," Matins said.

"So who did it?"

"The ex-husband."

"That easy?"

"That easy."

"Who was murdered?"

"Now, I can't tell you that."

Normally at this point in the game he'd laugh because he'd done it, tricked her again into a direct question. But he wasn't smiling; that unnerved her. John was a hardened professional. He'd worked sixteen years with the state police before running for sheriff. He was never flippant about local tragedies, but was not easily upset by them either. Why so grim? She looked at him, confused.

"No, Molly, really. This time I can't tell you."

"But why?"

"It'd be too personal for you."

"The victim is someone I know?"

"I don't know, but the murderer is."

Gone was any attempt at subtlety. "Who? You can't do this to me—I'll call the police."

"Molly, I *am* the police." Matins did have two deputies, but both worked most of the time as furniture movers, so basically, he was right about that; he was the police.

"I'll open your henhouse door to Goldie."

"Goldie would just chase them, not eat them."

Molly kept thinking. "I'll have a loud party. All night."

"I'll break it up; arrest everybody."

She thought frantically; what was the most awful thing she

could threaten him with? "Ah, I know," she said, narrowing her eyes, "I'll get Dr. K to do a study of rural crime."

That one gave Matins pause. A professional sociologist was so tiresome. He stood up, shifting from one lean leg to the other. He fiddled with his John Deere cap, bit his lip. Matins did wear a sheriff's shirt; rumor had it he owned a sheriff's hat, but he never wore it, preferring the cap. The rest of his outfit, jeans, hunting boots, silver buckle, was authority enough to suit him. His drawled reply if anyone chided his appearance was always, "I'm the duly elected sheriff; if I arrest someone, they're arrested whether I've got on a silly hat or not."

He was as thin as the day he left high school, but his face was lined and seamed from years of farming and hunting and smiling. He looked stern when he wasn't smiling, but he smiled too readily for the sternness pose to stick. The lines around his mouth had begun to twitch. He's weakening, Molly thought.

"Molly, this is going to upset you a whole bunch, but I guess you'll want to know. Promise me you'll stay out of it," he said.

"I always stay out of it."

Matins snorted. She stayed out of things about the same way Goldie stayed out of his chicken yard. "It's Dave. Dave Breyers. He killed Cathy, his ex."

Molly sat, stunned, staring sightlessly at her list, snacks and laundry forgotten. Now she understood why John was trying to protect her feelings.

"Impossible," she said finally.

"I'm sorry—got it all, opportunity, motive—"

"No," she interrupted, "that was the friendliest divorce in the history of breakups."

"She caught him embezzling—Molly, that's confidential. I haven't told you that. I've got to go; keep that damn dog home."

Goldie wagged appreciatively. With Matins, she thought "damn dog" was her name.

"Embezzling from whom?" But Matins was gone, slipping back into the woods toward his house.

3

LOUELLA

Molly was upset the rest of the morning. Not Dave. She drove to her Meal Van appointments, conversed convincingly with clients, but didn't really hear anything.

She glanced as usual at passing ridges and hills, but didn't see anything either. The late August wildflowers were thick in the ditches and pastures—ironweed, of course, tall and purple; goatsbeard, its taupe feathers fluttering in the wind; goldenrod; orange butterfly weed; the pale blue cornflower. Thickest of all was the Queen Anne's lace, its stately white umbels crocheting the fields. A hint of color in the dogwoods and staghorn sumacs promised an early fall. But Molly, usually so attuned to this, the beauty of the southern Ohio highlands, drove blindly, grieving.

She found herself feeling short tempered, driving carelessly, running stop signs—although on back roads she normally ran stop signs—but. But, that was it. Something terrible had happened and here she was—and here the whole thoughtless world was—going about its mundane routines as if everything were normal. Hi, how are are you? Fine? Think it'll rain? The oppressive normality of her day was infuriating.

Usually she was glad when she had to drive. The meals program had grown too large for her to drive much anymore. But today all she could do was think about Dave. She owed him a lot. Among other things, it was Dave who, fourteen years ago, had suggested she call his cousin, Patsy Bonneau, and volunteer to help the fledgling Meal Van project. At that time it consisted of Patsy and her station wagon. Today the Tricounty Meal Van Service had six trucks equipped with hot and cold units. Currently they delivered ninety-six hot meals at midday to seniors and shut-ins. The meals, once cooked in Patsy's or Molly's kitchen, were now prepped and packed from a remodeled kitchen in a former elementary school.

The school also had offices with touch-them-they're-real desks for Patsy, Molly and their new cook, Betty Matins. So what if they had to share the school with Head Start, the Southern Ohio Food Bank, WIC (Women, Infants and Children) and the Child Support Enforcement Agency. It was still a huge improvement over their former office in Patsy's laundry cupboard.

The price for such professionalism had been high, though. True, the top workers now had salaries. Patsy was full time and Molly and Betty were part time. But Patsy, who used to cook and drive, now spent most of her time sweet-talking state and federal bureaucrats or legislators for funding (or to overlook a regulation or two). She designed fund drives and special projects (such as the fair booth), plus she procured (i.e., begged for) food, planned the menus and trained drivers in safe food handling and good client relations. "We bring fellowship as well as food," Patsy taught their volunteers. "Talk to people, don't just hand them their trays."

Molly thought her job, as associate director, was more fun. She kept the books, wrote grant applications, maintained clients' records, arranged the volunteer cooks' or drivers' schedules and saw to it that the trucks were serviced and repaired. Sometimes this meant changing the oil herself; more often though she got Patsy's son, Peter, or her own son, Todd, to do it. She also interviewed potential clients in their homes. These interviews she especially liked. As needed, she helped Patsy with menu planning and special projects. But she missed the old days when, like Patsy, she cooked and drove.

Now she drove only in emergencies. The emergency this week was a driver had called in sick. No surprise there; the Lutherans were providing volunteers this month. The two women had discovered that Lutherans were sicker than anybody, even atheists. Their atheist volunteers almost never missed a day.

Molly told Ken she'd never take the Meal Van directorship even though Patsy offered it to her about once a week. She liked meeting clients and exploring remote scenic roads too much. The rugged landscape came not from ancient mountain folding, as did the real Appalachians farther east, but from a rush of melting water at the end of the Wisconsin ice age, which gouged the sandstone flats near the Ohio River into ridges and rock formations as exotic as any in the more photographed Southwest.

Before the glaciers, the area had been invaded several times by a retreating ocean, causing massive vegetation dieoffs. These were now seams of coal, visible as black stripes in the cliffsides Molly passed, but the coal was so sulfurous it was unsalable, contributing to the poverty of the area. The three counties served by the Meal Van were small but still had over two thousand miles of roads, although the sticky mash of tar, gravel and clay used for surfacing often seriously distorted the concept of "road."

Roads had evolved where settlers, Shawnee or deer had once walked, so some wound in dizzy series of hairpin loops along razorback ridges, and others plunged straight down into swampy, flood-prone hollows. Molly had become adept at driving these horrors, able to squish through mud, brake on gravel or descend tracks so steep the county had built "runaway truck lanes" for out-of-control vehicles to use for slowing down.

When family and friends back in Chicago blanched at using these roads to visit her, she explained it was easy, just like driving on ice, don't brake too hard, don't steer too quickly. "I don't find driving on ice easy," her brother would growl and he also would rent a car for visits now, rather than submit his precious Buick to the pings and furrows of back-country gravel.

Each road twisted and turned so erratically, Molly could count on getting lost every time she had to find a new client. She secretly enjoyed this. Being lost was how she found pre-Civil War cemeteries, abandoned log cabins, undiscovered Adena Indian mounds or, occasionally, whole ghost towns. Most roads were named for the settlers who first beat them into footpaths. At the moment, Molly was taking the riotous curves of Chalmers Ridge to deliver a meal to her last, most remote, and grouchiest client, Louella Chalmers Benton.

Louella was a coal miner's widow partly housebound by arthritis and maybe in her mid-seventies. Louella was proud she had been born in the county, even prouder that her mother, grandmother, great-grandmother and great-great-grandmother were also. Her ancestors on the Chalmers side had been in the county before it was legal, actually. Whites were forbidden to settle the area before the Revolutionary War because of a treaty with Shawnee Chief Cornstalk in 1774, which gave southern Ohio to the Shawnee if they agreed to leave Kentucky and Virginia settlers alone and to stop burning flatboats on the Ohio River.

At the treaty signing, the soldiers declared they supported the First Continental Congress. Since most tribes, including the Shawnee, later sided with the British, Louella argued this made Cornstalk's battles the first in the War for Independence, coming seven months before Lexington and Concord. So far Massachusetts had ignored her claim, as they had her mother, grandmother and great-grandmother before her. Whites abused the treaty, of course. Over thirty thousand of them, including a few Chalmerses, lived along the south bank of the Ohio River in 1774; fewer than twenty thousand Indians—all the Shawnee to the south plus the Delaware and Wynadot to the north—lived in the entire Ohio Country. Squatters saw nothing to stop them except savages who in their view ought to be exterminated anyway. Atrocities multiplied. Louella claimed to have lost so many ancestors to scalping during these years, Molly wondered how any had been left alive to forebear her—until Louella added she had Shawnee ancestry too. Chief Cornstalk himself, she bragged.

Louella's colorful heritage intimidated Molly until one day in self-defense she described her own great-grandfather, a Confederate private who had deserted at the first opportunity and fled to Illinois, promising never to bear arms again against the Union.

Louella was impressed. In this region, she explained, respectable ancestors, governors and senators and such, were of no account. Notorious ancestors, however—that was different. A cowardly grandfather was just fine. How about horse thieves? Did Molly have any horse thieves in her past? Louella wanted to know. That conversation was the beginning of a grudging friendship for the two women.

Molly pulled into Louella's yard, stepped to the back of the truck to assemble the hot meal and started to the porch. Louella was waiting, frowning sourly. Her frown made her seem larger than her four foot eleven. She was a thin, well-kept woman in a bright calico dress, with a high mound of white hair which she frequently touched, unconsciously emphasizing the swollen joints of her hands.

"You git lost again?" Louella complained.

"No," Molly said.

"Yore late."

"I know." It had been a long time since Molly had bothered saying she was sorry to Louella, mainly because she knew the woman's nastiness was a ploy to get apologies.

"I had something on my mind," Molly said, "so I forgot to drive like a bat out of hell."

Louella pretended to be offended, but in truth she loved bad words, and Molly knew it. Swear for the woman, yes. Apologize for her, no.

"I'll jist bet you ha' the news on your mind," Louella said, opening the door for Molly. The house was a four-room miner's shack, with the traditional pointed roof, center chimney, porch and eight windows. It was in good repair, with indoor plumbing; one of the two bedrooms had been converted into a bath. Except for some sills needing paint and a slight sag to the porch, everything inside and out was neat. The couch and chair in the living room were covered with old bedspreads to keep them clean. Every table had a crocheted doily cover. Every surface, from tables to lamps to Louella's ceramic cat collection, was spotless.

"Yes, I've been thinking about the news," Molly said.

"Whut make hit so strange," Louella said, "is't Slim Coolis don't have no goats."

"What? What are you talking about?" said Molly.

"On the radio this morning. Slim Coolis supposed to 'a had three billies and seeing how he don't have a nanny hit's a miracle," said Louella. She laughed. "No nanny and three billies."

"Well, actually I was thinking more about the news of the murder," Molly said.

"Sich a shame. Poor Cathy, that gal who got herself kilt, is a grandniece of'n mine," Louella said.

"Was," Molly said, wondering how Louella knew details already. Wrongbutton hadn't mentioned names on his newscast. "Really? Your niece?"

Louella sniffed at the impertinence of the question. "I not only ha' nieces, I ha' children. Up north," she said.

"Well, so do I," Molly started to say, but caught herself. Sparring with Louella would gain her nothing.

"What was Cathy like?" she said instead.

"She'd been a good girl."

"What do you mean?"

"Well, she never say 'bat outta you know where.' "

"Was she married?" Molly had learned that success in Appalachian conversation sometimes meant asking a question she knew the answer to—to see if her source were truthful.

"Well, that so-called husband of her'n don't count."

"Why not?"

"Jist knew it woun'ta worked."

"Why not?"

"Just woun't is't all. Kin I ha' my lunch now?"

Molly sighed. Appalachian etiquette. She'd lost. She'd been too direct, so Louella wouldn't tell her anything. Unlike Matins, Louella strictly enforced the rules. But what did Louella know? Molly figured it would be days before she'd even find out when Louella had last seen Cathy. The battle of wills was joined, and both women knew it. Molly smiled sweetly at the old woman, handed her the lunch and told her she would see her tomorrow.

Louella smiled triumphantly back.

4
POWERS

With the county fair still a day and a half away, Molly expected the fairgrounds to be deserted, but the parking lot was jammed, the rides were nearly assembled, the campground was full of trailers and kids ran everywhere. Through the bustle, Molly saw Patsy, talking as usual, by the door of the Exhibit Hall.

Patsy saw her, waved her over. "Here, over here," she boomed. Patsy's voice was built for crowds, a good thing, because Patsy herself was small and easily overlooked otherwise. She wore a casual denim skirt and T-shirt, but managed to make them look elegant with her perfectly trimmed hair and hand-beaded earrings. She habitually fingered her reading glasses, hung about her neck on a chain, also hand-beaded. Patsy Bonneau had one of the few French surnames in the Tricounty. She was descended from a party of aristocrats who had fled the French Revolution. Although many French nobles came to Ohio to escape the guillotine, few stayed, because the frontier was too uncomfortable. No servants, no decent roads, no powder for their wigs. Patsy said her forebears stayed not from toughness, but inertia. They were sloshing along in the wilderness when Patsy's great-great-

great-grandmother sat down one afternoon and refused to move. She'd had enough of this nonsense and here they'd stay, she'd said. So they did.

Whatever the inertia of her ancestors, none of it had been passed on to Patsy. She was tireless. A vibrant, funny woman, her face was constantly mobile, every thought registering on it before she spoke. The trait made her an irresistible recruiter. Hunger was her cause. Anyone who hadn't volunteered after talking with her was incredibly strong willed. Even her son, Peter, who at the moment stood behind her seething with boredom, got roped into spending many of his weekends helping her. Peter's father, Andrew McDaniel, was minister at the Church of Christ. The couple were divorced, but friendly. Patsy had to be nice to her ex; his church provided twice as many Meal Van volunteers as any church in the area.

The women Patsy was talking to held dried flower arrangements, entries for the fair, they said as Patsy introduced them.

"Our booth is between the end of baked goods and the start of fresh vegetables," Patsy said when they had left.

"Is that good?"

"It's great. Everyone, I mean everyone, checks out both. The fiercest competitions at the fair, after livestock, are garden vegetables and baked goods."

"I can't believe how many people are here."

"They can't unload their animals without a vet check and rule is they have to be in place by nine A.M. tomorrow. So everyone's here today, especially the vets."

"Full campgrounds. I'd never even noticed there were campgrounds here before."

Patsy looked startled. "Don't you come to the fair each year?"

"Yes, of course. Well, just for the rides and the horse races."

"You've missed the real fair, then. The ribbons—that's what fairs are for. Charlotte Bannich's going to miss the gardening contests this year because of her knee surgery. Won't be the same without her since she wins so much. Remind me to talk to you about Charlotte later; she's going to need some meals from us. Oh look, there's Tom Powers." Patsy started waving and Peter groaned. Would his mother never be done yakking and get this booth done so he could get back to campus?

"Who?" Molly said.

"Tom Powers. You know, 'Thank you, Mr. Chicken Man.'"

"Oh no. Patsy. Don't . . ."

"Mr. Powers. Here's Molly. I want you to meet her," Patsy bellowed.

Molly watched in dismay as Powers bounded over. He raised chickens and was one of the few prosperous farmers in the Tricounty. Three months ago he'd donated twenty chickens to the Meal Van. Twenty *live* chickens. Betty had been furious. None of the volunteer cooks would, um, "dress" the birds, as the euphemism went, so Betty, Molly and Patsy had spent an awful afternoon in the school's parking lot whacking off heads and plucking feathers. Betty groused for days because not only were the birds live, they were old, stewing chickens at best, not fryers. Molly still got queasy thinking about that day and wondered what kind of outrageous tax deduction he would claim for dumping those birds on them.

Powers, short, stocky and balding, smiled broadly. A wedding band pinched the flesh of his pudgy left hand; a signet ring cut the pinky of his right. He dressed like a merchant, not a farmer, in chinos, white short-sleeved shirt and tie—except for his feet. There he wore chore boots, those ugly green rubbers sold only on back racks in farm stores. Molly had a pair for garden work, but she had never, ever seen anyone wear them in public before.

"Well, hello, hello," he beamed. "Can you use more chickens?"

"Why thank you, Mr. Powers," Patsy smoothly beamed back, "but I'm afraid we can't. The health inspector told us not to take any more donations. It's the law. I didn't know, but all our food has to be processed and then inspected."

No food inspector had been by; Patsy, getting into her lie, began to embellish. "Bureaucrats. Always causing us trouble. It's just not fair, but what am I to do?" She shrugged, real pain on her face. How that Patsy could lie, Molly thought; always with conviction. The best lies, Patsy liked to say, are almost true. "But what brings you to the fair so early?"

"I'm judging the poultry competition, so I have to help the vet inspect the birds for disease before we let them into the barn," Powers said.

Molly was surprised. "A poultry competition?"

"Six to be exact, all to be judged Saturday."

"Do you have that many entries?"

"We've had so many we've had to convert half the Cattle Barn to a poultry barn. Poultry are real popular this year."

Now it was Patsy's turn to be surprised. "Any idea why?"

"No idea."

"I don't remember seeing you here before," Patsy said. "Have you judged before?"

"My, yes, usually every other year. I switch off with Cathy Breyers; this was her year to judge."

Both women gasped. "Such an awful thing. Do you know any details?"

Powers shrugged. "Haven't seen the paper yet."

Patsy then saw someone else she knew and was waving again. Molly seized the moment to rescue Peter. "Let's go build a booth," she said.

"Somebody ought to." He laughed. "She'll talk all day." Molly and Peter knew from long experience that Patsy would greet people for hours. If the booth were to be done in time, they'd have to do it. Molly didn't mind. Patsy's gift of gab translated directly into volunteers and gifts for the Meal Van. The two began pleating a cloth around their table.

"So what courses are you taking this term?" Molly asked.

"Dr. K's Appalachian Culture is one. We've met twice this

week. I think I'm going to like it. It's not just reading and tests. We have to do a service project."

"Yes, he does that every year." Molly liked Peter; he was always enthusiastic. Younger than her own son, Todd, he'd been like a little brother for Todd, and had adopted Molly as a second mother.

"Has Patsy conned you into working the booth this weekend?"

"She's trying to." Peter laughed. The two sorted photographs Patsy had brought and were pinning them to the board behind the table when Molly heard a snort behind her. She turned to see Louella, held up by a cane on one side and a sturdy grandniece on the other.

"Yer pictures ain't straight," Louella criticized.

"They're not meant to be," Molly said.

"I think they'da look better straight."

"Well, we'll think about it. It's nice to see you out. What brings you here?"

"I've entered the table centerpiece contest. Over thar. Care to look?"

"Why, of course." Three centerpieces occupied the table. Cattails, baby's breath, statice and she couldn't tell what all else filled their hopeful vases.

"Rules are they's supposed to be found objects, nat'rally dried plants, not boughten, but sometimes thar's cheating."

"Which one's yours?"

"Number 427."

"Why is it number 427 if there are only three here?"

"That's how many since 1951, when the fair board started numbering, though the fair's been agoin' since 1846, 'cept, o' course, fer the War."

"World War Two?"

"No, the Civil War."

"Did numbers for all contests start in 1951?"

"All them I enter."

"All?"

"Well, I cain't do as many as I uster, but I git on four or five each year."

Molly looked now over the whole hall. Most of the tables were still bare, awaiting entries, but the signs were in place: Floral Arrangements, Dried. Floral Arrangements, Fresh. Hanging Baskets, Foliage. Hanging Baskets, Floral. Corsages. Infant Layette, Crocheted. Infant Layette, Knitted. Sweaters with Sleeves, Crocheted. Sweaters with Sleeves, Knitted. Gloves or Mittens, Knitted or Crocheted. Afghans, Knitted. Afghans, Crocheted. Shawls, Crocheted or Knitted. Quilts, Pieced. Quilts, Embroidered. Quilts, Appliquéd. Yeast Breads, White. Yeast Rolls, Cinnamon. Yeast Rolls, Pecan. Baking Powder Biscuits. Zucchini Bread. Cookies, Molded. Cookies, Drop. Cakes, Chocolate. Cakes, Upside Down. Cakes, Decorated (cake required). Table Cloths, Embroidered. Table Cloths, Crocheted. Candlewicking. Candles, Handmade. Teddybears, Handmade . . .

And many more too far away to read. The whole invisible world of women spread on tables, she thought. Were all county fairs like this one? How many hundreds of fairs in hundreds of countries were there? How many women have come together in places like this to compete and share secrets? How long have there been fairs? Since medieval times? Since biblical times?

She thought of the shows her parents took her to as a girl. The Chicago Auto Show. The Home and Energy Show. Taste of Chicago. International Gems and Jewelry. Chicago Ski and Travel. Those were, she was realizing, places where you learned what you could buy. But here, where people took care of themselves, you learned what you could do. Skills, not consumption, were celebrated here. And women were the driving force, the leaders, quietly, one stitch or recipe at a time, building civilizations. And had been doing so for generations, for millennia.

"How many contests are there?" she said, awed.

"Over twelve hundred," said another voice. "Thirty-eight just for zinnias alone. Hi, I'm Frances Jamison; I manage the exhibits. I saw you working on the Meal Van booth. I like what you've done with the pictures."

Molly smiled. "Thank you," she said, carefully avoiding Louella's eyes.

"Tell Patsy I have some 4-H girls who will staff the booth most of the time, but you'll need to have someone here on Saturday."

"Right." Poor Peter, she thought.

Patsy was still talking to acquaintances as she left the hall. Molly nodded her goodbyes. Peter had slipped out another door. Molly was thinking about her vision in the hall as she walked toward the parking lot. Just when she felt she was beginning to understand these people she would see something like this which both opened her eyes and deepened her puzzlement. Rural people were not like urban folk. Maybe Betty was right; you were a newcomer until you'd been here fifty years.

5

BUTCHER

Out of the corner of her eye, Molly noticed the Cattle Barn. Cathy's world, she thought. She'd never known Cathy as she did Dave. It was always Dave out front at Breyers Mill. Cathy would be in the back fiddling with her computer or sorting the stock. Even if Dave were busy with customers, Cathy never came out. Would she talk to no one? Who was she? On impulse, Molly turned to the barn. Maybe a sense of the woman was inside that barn.

She passed a boy who was vigorously soaping a steer he'd chained to a spigot by the barn. A hand-lettered sign on the north side of the building said POULTRY. Inside, cattle of all sizes filled the stalls of the south half. People sat in webbed lawn chairs in the aisle. Radios, picnic chests, portable electronic games and CD players littered the laps and ground around the people who loitered in the aisle. She even saw a couple of rolled-up sleeping bags.

They're guarding their cattle, Molly thought, shocked. Vaguely she recalled now the many newspaper stories of people sabotaging fair animals. No shotguns, she noted gratefully. Probably a rule of the fair. As she walked through the barn, she collected a fresh appreciation for the wisdom of Tom Powers' chore boots. On the poultry side, tables had been set up in the stalls, with three or four cages per table. Again, people sat in lawn chairs surrounded by snacks and diversions, guarding their animals.

Powers stood at one table surrounded by a dozen children. Beside him was a young man afflicted with Down syndrome. Butcher Cook. Molly knew Butcher. He lived in the County Home, a halfway house for people who could partly take care of themselves. He worked part time for a mowing service which specialized in hiring the less abled. This is how Molly knew him; he helped with the grass at the school building each week. When he first started working, the mower had baffled him, but his supervisors were skilled in teaching methods. "The secret," one had told Molly, "is task analysis. With a normal person, if I told you to get in a swimming pool and you'd never done it, you'd figure it out; but the retarded have to be taught step by step: walk over to the pool edge, sit on the edge, put your toes in the water, slide into the water but hold on to the side—that one's hard; it's two things at once. And each step has to be practiced over and over, but they can learn real well; it just takes patience."

One thing Butcher had to practice over and over at first was going backward with the mower. He could go forward easily enough, but it took him a long time to remember to pull back on the mower if he came to an obstacle. Once he got it, though, he worked hard with almost no supervision. Butcher's favorite tool was the leaf blower used to clear sidewalks of grass clippings. If given it, he would not stop blowing. No amount of persuasion worked—he didn't or chose not to understand the idea "done," so the supervisors finally started putting only a small amount of gas in the machine. They told Butcher the machine was "tired" when it stopped and had to rest until their next stop. Many a time Molly had come back to her office to see the other workers sitting in the truck smoking, all mowing done, while they waited for Butcher to run out of gas.

No one knew Butcher's real name. His nickname came from his life before the Human Services Agency found him living alone in an abandoned cabin in the woods, where he survived by harvesting and cooking roadkill. They brought him out of the woods and put him in the home, much to Butcher's delight. It was a surprise to him that there were other Down's adults. Meanwhile, debate raged through the Tricounty for weeks about him. Who'd left him there? Whose child was he? Why hadn't anyone known about him? The director of Human Services said he must have been brought and abandoned by someone from another county or they'd have known of him, but the chief of the Tricounty Mental Health Board countered that given the stigma some families still attached to handicapped children, it's possible a family had kept him hidden all these years.

Whatever his origins, he had been well cared for. Worldwide, experts on Down syndrome agree that early at-home care and teaching improves the potential of these children. Someone had lovingly done this because Butcher was quite accomplished, considering. He could talk, manage his personal hygiene, dress himself and—as his nickname attested—feed himself. That meant, as with the mower, someone had broken those skills down into tiny steps and taught him over and over. But who? And why abandon him? If asked, Butcher just said his parents were dead; their names, he'd say, were Mom and Dad.

Judge Gains, who'd ruled Butcher was competent to live at the halfway house under the guardianship of Human Services, speculated that his parents or caregivers had gotten too old or poor or ill to cope anymore and had abandoned him where he could be found. This way they could avoid admitting their "shame." A pity, the judge had told the newspaper, with such stigmas a prejudice of the past.

Butcher saw Molly, recognized her and hastened over to talk. It was hard to tell how old he was since a trait of Down's people is rapid aging. He looked about thirty-five but he could have been as young as twenty. He was typically short, about five feet, with small hands, stubby fingers, flat nose, short neck, folded ears and the slanting eyes that hallmark the condition. But his diction was good, compared to others like him, unless he became excited and tried to talk rapidly. Then it was hard to understand him. He walked with a rolling gait, heavy on the left, which made Molly wonder if he also had another trait not unusual for Down's, a deformed foot.

His personality was likewise typical, although it infuriated the director of the County Home for anyone to call her beloved charges typical. "We are still recovering from the harm done by Langdon Down, who stereotyped them as loving, imitative imbeciles. They are individuals, not patterns," she would say. But the fact was, individual or no, Butcher was everything Molly had ever heard of Down's adults—cheerful, friendly, outgoing, active, a little boisterous sometimes, and as with the leaf blower, sometimes stubborn.

"Meals lady," Butcher said. "I like chicken."

"Do you? How are you, Butcher?" Molly said. She thought it was odd he was here with Powers.

"I eat chicken every day. It's good."

"Do you eat these chickens?" Molly asked.

"Not yet," Butcher said. "Mr. Powers, he tells me."

"He tells you what?" Molly said.

"He tells me about good chickens."

Molly walked over to Powers, Butcher walking behind her bragging about his recent good eatings. Molly heard the word "muskrat" and then "possum," then tried valiantly to ignore him. Powers was holding a small brown rooster with long silken feathers. Its feet were completely feathered, she noticed with surprise.

Powers talked in a pompous tone that irritated Molly, but the children were intent. "How are you supposed to dress for the judging on Saturday? Does anyone know?" Powers asked.

One boy waved his hand. "I know. All in white. All in white."

"That's right; that's the showmanship tradition. Wear white. Now, how do you hold your birds?"

The children were silent. "Like this, like a baby, in your left arm." He handed the bird to one of the girls. "In your left, that's right. Now stroke the bird to keep him calm. Good. Now, when I say 'Show me the wing,' how do you do that?"

The girl tried to open the wing. "No," Powers said. "I'll show you. You grab the main joint in the wing. It's like a backwards elbow. Now gently push on the point of this elbow and hold the bottom feathers and just pull, pull, like this, pull, until you see all the feathers. Now, when I say 'Show the feet,' you take the foot, put your finger in the center and spread all the toes, like this. When I say 'Show me the other side,' switch the bird to the other arm and do the same thing. Just like this."

Molly was fascinated. She wondered if Cathy had spent time teaching the children as Powers was. She couldn't imagine it. Powers continued his coaching. "On Saturday I'm going to ask you questions. Do you know what kind of bird you have?"

"Good bird. Yum," Butcher said. The children laughed.

"What breed is this?" Powers repeated. The boy who owned the bird shrugged.

"It's a Buff Cochin. They came from China in about 1850. Some people call them Shanghais. I'm going to ask you about the parts of the bird. What's this?" He pointed to the breast.

"White meat," Butcher shouted.

"This is the keel. What's this?" He pointed to the fleshy mass under the beak. "It's a wattle. And this?" He pointed to the comb. Molly was surprised the children didn't know that one. Even as a city girl, she knew the comb.

Just then, Powers noticed Molly listening. "Oh hi," he said. "Do your kids have a bird in the show?"

"No," she said, "my children are grown. They don't keep animals anymore. I had no idea there was so much to poultry judging."

"Well, Cathy and I have worked hard to improve the poultry shows here in the Tricounty. It's hard, though. Poultry is the poor folks' hobby. They can't afford cattle or sheep, so they get a bird for their children. But they don't know anything about showmanship or breeding. So their children aren't prepared for the judging."

Molly glanced again at the people in the barn. She knew from her years of working for the Meal Van that poverty was physical. Poor people tended to be too thin or too fat, and she saw that in the barn now. The people guarding the cattle had normal bodies. The people by the poultry did not. Tom saw her glance. "Yes, top prize for Best of Show in the poultry division is only $300. The cattle division Best of Show could be auctioned off for eight or nine thousand. Still, for a poor family, that $300 prize is worth the trouble of competing."

"These birds are beautiful," Molly said.

"It's a hobby of mine," he said. "Cathy Breyers sells—I mean sold—I wonder if Dave will keep marketing these breeds now. Most of the birds here came from Breyers Mill. Look, here's a Phoenix." He took out a bird with a long, sweeping silver and black tail. "These come from Japan and were once only allowed to be kept by the emperor." He handed the bird to Butcher, who with surprising skill put it back in its cage.

"Now here is a Silver Gray Dorking." Powers took out another silver and black bird, but with shorter feathers. "This is an old breed. It was introduced to Britain by the Romans in about 125 A.D., but was old even then. It's unusual for its fifth toe and short legs. Most chickens have only four toes." He handed this bird to Butcher too, who gently stroked it.

"Now, here's a bird I like," Powers said.

Molly read the sign on the cage aloud: "White-crested Black Polish." She pronounced it like furniture polish.

"No, Polish as in Poland. The bird comes from Poland, but they were popular throughout Europe. You see them in sixteenth-century Dutch paintings."

The bird was all black except for an explosion of white feathers on its head which looked something like a Dolly Parton wig.

"I've never seen anything like these before," Molly said.

"They're fun, aren't they," Powers said.

"Did Cathy know as much as you about poultry?"

"Oh, yes, we're in the business, you know. I raise fryers and eggs. She sells day-olds."

"Day-olds?" Molly said.

"Yes, chicks that have just been hatched and not fed yet, although I think sometimes she fed them."

"I know Dave really well," Molly said, "but I'm beginning to realize I didn't know Cathy at all."

"Anyone in poultry knew her. She was an expert."

"What was she like as a person?"

"Kind of hard to know, very shy. If you didn't have something to say about chickens, there wasn't much to talk about with Cathy."

"I like chickens," Butcher said.

"Why would anyone want to kill her?" Molly said.

Powers frowned as he put the Polish bird back in its cage. "I have no idea."

"Roosters are good to eat," Butcher said.

6

DAVE

Driving home, Molly passed Dave Breyers' trailer. His truck was in the drive. She braked, backed into the yard and sat. She didn't expect him to be there. To her surprise, he opened the door for her. "I thought on such a nice day you would take your motorcycle to work," she lied.

"Decided to take the day off," he lied in return. He looked tired. He was about average height, thin, even scrawny, with straight, longish black hair. Most of her neighbors were slightly shaggy. Only students could afford regular barbering. Dave's black hair, pale skin and green eyes reflected his Welsh heritage. Like Louella, he knew his ancestors, which in their way were as notorious as hers. The Welsh had come during the mining boom of the 1860s. One of his great-great-uncles had helped push a burning coal car into a mine shaft during the violent New Straitsville strike of 1884. This fire was still burning underground more than a century later. Most of the immigrants into southern Ohio in the mid-nineteenth century were Scotch-Irish, but in the Tricounty area, a significant group of Welsh had settled. Dave said he thought Breyers was a corruption of a

Welsh name Brywedd. Some Brywedds were buried in a cemetery by his church.

Dave lived about eight farms from the Wests'. By country standards that made him a neighbor, especially since as the itinerant crow flew, Dave was next to them on the side opposite from the sheriff although their woods were larger than Matins'. A huge wing-shaped chunk of the Wayne National Forest separated their homes, but despite the size of that barrier, Dave had been the first neighbor Molly had gotten to know when she and Ken had first moved to the county from Chicago. Her kids, Todd and Amanda, had been eight and ten then. Dr. K was a new assistant professor at the college.

It was Dave who gave Dr. K his nickname. He'd been just plain Kenneth then, but since another Dr. Kenneth West was the pediatrician in town, a new name was needed. So Dr. K. Old Dr. West had long since retired and left the area, but almost everyone (even Molly sometimes) still called him Dr. K.

She had met Dave one afternoon when she and the kids were hiking in the forest. Impulsively she invited him and "the wife" over for dinner. Dave came; Cathy didn't. "She's not feeling well," he apologized. Molly would learn in the years thereafter that Cathy never felt well enough to accept social invitations. Molly had met Cathy at home only once when she took some homemade bread over to their trailer as a thank-you present to Dave for his helping cut up some fallen trees. Cathy had been very abrupt, not inviting her in, not thanking her for the bread. Molly had been shocked. True, newcomers, especially those at the college, were resented by local people. But rarely were the natives out-and-out rude.

At dinner that first night, conversation had turned to how much Molly missed working. She hadn't been able to find anything, she complained. Benefits at the college were handled by a woman who also ran a convenience and bait shop with her husband. Payroll was administered by another part-time worker who sharpened chain saws on the side. There was nothing, nothing at all for someone like her.

That's when Dave told her about the Meal Van.

Molly thanked him later, telling him she'd found a new life, plus a world she'd never imagined. Dr. K might be teaching sociology, but she lived it, she'd said.

She stood looking at Dave now. Fourteen years. He'd taught her kids to ride horseback. He'd helped bushhog their pasture. Replace gutters. Fix mowers. Haul injured kids to the emergency room or pets to the vet. He was neighborliness personified. This man could not murder.

"Have you slept at all?" she said.

"You know?"

"Of course."

"You want a beer?"

"Sure."

"On the deck or inside?"

"Outside." Molly sat on Dave's deck while he got the beers. The view overlooked a series of ridges each smoothed by pastures. The national forest between their homes was behind the trailer. In front, the fields were beginning to shimmer with a humid haze. By dusk the haze would be fog. The sounds, like the wildflowers, were peculiar to late August, the thrum of locusts, the intermittent spurts of angry cicadas, the high trilling of crickets and tree frogs. It was a harmonious cacophony loud enough to be audible above the country music station Dave had on inside.

The pastures were mown in strips that softly contoured the ridge lines. When the Shawnee hunted this land it was all woods except for occasional meadows, which the tribes kept clear by burning. James Smith, a Shawnee captive/adoptee, described hunting for deer one morning in a meadow: "We met with some Ottawa hunters, and agreed to take what they call a ring hunt, in partnership. We waited until we expected rain was near falling to extinguish the fire, and then we kindled a large circle in the prairie. A great number of deer lay concealed in the grass but as the fire burned in towards the center of the circle, the deer fled before the fire. Indians shot them down every opportunity."

Nowadays the meadows were kept clear by haying, but with a chronic recession in cattle, more land was returning to forest. The state helped by funding reforestry projects for the whole southern tier of counties. In the fifteen years the Wests had lived in the area, the view in front of their own home had disappeared behind a mix of sycamores, sassafrases, poplars and conifers. The view at Dave's had filled in to the right. Dave handed her the beer. "Too many trees?"

"You can never have too many trees." Molly didn't know what to ask first. How do you talk to a friend suspected of murdering a woman who was both his ex-wife and current business partner? Dave and Cathy had bought a falling-down 150-year-old mill site at the edge of town when they married, and turned the mill into a tourist attraction and the granary buildings into a feed, horse tack, pet, garden and hummingbird supply center. Like most businesses in this region it couldn't survive by specializing. People came from miles around to look at the offbeat hummingbird feeders or to watch the water-powered stone grinding corn. They returned to take advantage of the prices on feed for dogs, goats, rabbits, ducks, wild birds, chickens, horses, pigs and cats. In the spring they came to buy the unusual breeds of chicks the mill stocked. The business had prospered for ten years when Dave and Cathy decided to divorce. They agreed to joint custody both of their daughter, Christy, and of their business—still to be called Breyers Mill.

"I know it's weird," Dave had said at the time, "but Cathy and I always worked well together. She's great at new products—the hummingbird gimmick is hers. And she manages the money well. Me, I'm the people person. I'm better at dealing with distributors, hiring and firing employees and handling customers.

We'd be crazy to break up the team." Later Dave told Molly the divorce was the best thing they'd ever done for each other and for the business. "We're good business partners, but lousy marriage partners." After a while people quit talking about it or even thinking it strange.

"I didn't expect you to be here," Molly said finally.

"They questioned me last night, and impounded my shotguns. But they can't hold you just on suspicion—they have to have evidence."

"Who found her?" Molly asked.

"Bill." Bill Winthrop was a local carpenter who didn't need ancestors to be notorious. He was famous for starting jobs and quitting before he finished. He, like everyone else in the Tri-county area, needed two jobs to survive. His other work was playing banjo and guitar in a local quasi-Cajun, sometimes country, on-a-whim rock band—repertoire designed to suit client. "He was fixing a wall in the back storeroom and found her."

"When?"

"Last night. About eight. It was him who called the sheriff. He'd come back to check the mud on the drywall, he said."

"How'd he react?"

"Predictable. He quit."

"Matins seemed pretty convinced you did it."

"That's his job—suspect the ex first."

"He thinks there's more to it."

"Like maybe I was embezzling from Cathy?"

"How could he think such a thing?" Molly said.

"Easy." Dave half laughed, half sobbed. "Real easy. You see, Molly, I *was* embezzling from her."

7
CRIME

The students, fourteen of them, arrived in twos and threes, some complaining of getting lost, some exclaiming about the beauty of the ridge, but most heading right for Goldie and the puppy. Students always seemed pet starved, Molly thought. Dr. K handed out nametags as they entered. It was the first week of classes, he apologized, so he didn't know names—but the sooner he and everyone learned them, the better the project.

"Sit anywhere," he said, pointing them to a living room decorated in a style their daughter, Amanda, always called Early Clutter. Plants hung in macramé holders, stained glass circles hung in windows. Pewter unicorns were salted among dozens of glass bottles. Some of the bottles were fine handblown glass, but just as many were cheap "collectibles." Photos occupied all other spaces not filled by bottles or unicorns. A tropical fish tank competed with bookcases for Best Textural Chaos award. Cushions of every color and pattern were stacked on the floor beside, under or, occasionally, on every chair. Molly defended the clutter as a good way to hide dust and pet hair. Or pets, her family would retort, since a dog or cat was more likely than a person

to be occupying a given piece of furniture. The students settled into this visual uproar comfortably, absorbed by the clutter like so many more cushions.

What kind of dogs were these, they wanted to know, and how old were they? They listened to the answers just long enough for politeness before beginning to describe their own dogs back home, which they seemed to miss more than parents or siblings. It was always a shock to be reminded how young students were, Molly thought. They looked and acted adult, but when they played with the dogs, Molly could see adolescence was just yesterday. No, it's today, Dr. K would reply, especially if papers were due. Goldie wriggled from student to student, delighted by the excess of affection. The puppy seemed baffled but happy.

"Is anybody allergic to dogs? If so, I'll put them out."

One student timidly raised a hand, risking glares from the others, but their disappointment was short-lived because then Peter Pan and Wendy, Molly's cats, sauntered through to check out not the students, but the food. The cat lovers in the group then got their turn to fuss and tell until Molly said, "Is anyone allergic?"

Again, one was. This time the others could not limit themselves to glares. Peter, who always said he was honored to have a cat named for him, pointed to Molly's tropical fish tank. "I hope no one's allergic to fish—that's too heavy to put outside."

As Molly dumped the cats out the door, Dr. K was finishing artistry on a veggie tray.

"Are you going to sit in?" he asked.

"For a little while maybe," she said.

"Is everybody here?"

"How many are you expecting?"

"Fifteen."

"All but one, then."

As Dr. K came in, chatter stopped. I could never get used to that, Molly thought, the way people act differently when a teacher enters a room. He seemed oblivious to the effect.

"Well, what shall we talk about?" he said.

Dead silence.

I'd go nuts, Molly thought; I'd babble immediately. But Dr. K waited patiently for something to happen.

"What sorts of projects have past classes done?" one student finally asked.

"We've had a literacy project, parenting classes for expectant teen mothers, a fundraiser for the Meal Van program—wonder where that idea came from?" Dr. K smiled at Molly. "A GED tutoring program for prisoners, a—"

"What's a GED program?"

"General equivalency diploma—high school diplomas for people who quit high school. Let's see what else—we started the Habitat for Humanity project in the Tricounty area and last year we tried an environmental project."

"What do you mean tried?"

"What's your name? Jenny. Well, Jenny, we wanted to do a survey of endangered plant species but landowners were reluctant to let us onto their land."

"Why?"

"I think some of them were growing unendangered illegal crops."

"Whoa? Marijuana?" said Peter, eyes widening.

"Yes."

"I hear of people being shot for hiking too close to hidden fields," said Peter.

"Someone was shot yesterday, a woman," said another student, named Marie.

"Could that have been a drug murder, Dr. K?" another asked.

"I don't know. Molly, what have you heard?"

"The paper said there was no apparent motive."

"Yes, but what have you heard?"

She thought for a second about Dave's confession, but said, "Nothing. No one seems to have a clue."

"Where was she found?"

"At the Mill, in a storeroom."

"I think it's terrible. One reason I chose a rural college was to get away from big-city crime," said nametag Eric.

"Rural crime is a bigger problem than you think, and it is increasing," said Dr. K.

"What kinds of crime?" Jenny wanted to know. Dr. K was beginning to notice she asked good questions.

"Vandalism is the number-one crime."

"Like mailbox bashing?" asked Peter.

"Was that you who did that, Peter?" There'd been a score of mailboxes destroyed one night the spring before.

"Me? Never. But students probably did; it is a regular fraternity initiation thing, drive out, whap some boxes."

The students laughed.

"Some of the vandalism is more sinister, carving occult symbols in grain fields, stuff like that," said Jenny.

"What other kinds of crime are there, Dr. K?"

"Let me think. After vandalism, there's—" He stopped, apparently looking at the floor but in reality accessing from one frontal lobe or the other.

"There's theft, that's next most common, especially of gasoline. Farmers keep a lot of fuel around for their machines. Next are auto offenses; no one in the country stops for stop signs. Then come threats."

"What kinds of threats?"

"All kinds, but mostly for violence. After that comes domestic crimes—fights, spouse abuse, that sort of thing."

"But why is it increasing?" Marie wanted to know.

"Many reasons," Dr. K began. He's getting warmed up, Molly thought.

"You have to look to the history and culture of rural areas to understand it. Appalachian culture in particular breeds a cavalier attitude toward crime. Rural crime is unlike urban crime in that it's much less social. We think crimes are individual, deviant acts. But in towns they can be social acts. By our standards shooting, stealing, etc., are very bad crimes, but there are some urban neighborhoods where you're nobody unless you've done time for something like that. Your social status comes from your community values, even if those values are violent. Sure, we read about this and think how awful. What we don't read about are the much more common community values *against* crime. 'Don't shoplift. Don't drive too fast. Don't drive off without paying for your gas.' Community values keep the lid on in towns."

"And keep the lawns mowed?" Eric laughed.

Marie said, "In some neighborhoods in Columbus putting your trash out on the wrong side of the curbside mailbox is against the law."

"Really?" Dr. K said. "That's wonderful; a perfect example of community values defining crime. But in rural areas there are no communities. There are neighbors, but that's not the same. So there are fewer social restraints on individuals. If you're inclined to steal or toss trash in the yard or let grass grow too tall or shoot someone, there's no community to hold you back.

"Another incentive for rural crime is its romantic tradition. West of the Appalachians, thieves or trespassers were seen as Indian fighters or frontiersmen opening the wilderness. Livestock rustling, moonshining, smuggling and racist crimes—better known to Hollywood as the cowboy and Indian movie—are rural, not urban crimes. Country crime has a romantic heritage.

"Even today, a strong Robin Hood idea lingers in the country. People believe law and government are hostile to the people. For most people this takes the form of petty scofflawing—running stop signs, letting dogs run loose"—he glanced toward Molly and grinned—"not reporting cash earned for labor, ignoring safety regulations, lying to get food coupons. Families here can't survive on one income. Sometimes that second income is mildly illegal. People feel they have a right to break the law to survive. Now the question is, how narrow is the gap between scofflaw and criminal? Do scofflaws move on to harder crimes?"

Several students shrugged, expecting him to answer. "I don't know; no one does. Rural crime needs to be studied a lot more by sociologists, most of whom, like the rest of society, live in cities. So there's not much research done on rural crime."

Ah, the social science mantra, Molly thought: More research is needed.

"I don't understand why it's increasing; there are fewer farmers now," said Eric.

"That's why. The distance between homes is greater than ever. Valuable equipment and grain tend to be stored in buildings far from farmhouses. Farmers and their wives have to work at town jobs to make ends meet, so no one's about during the day. And they're victimized because they're good churchgoers. One of the most popular times for stealing is Wednesday night when people are at midweek service."

The students laughed, but Molly started thinking. This was Thursday. So last night, when Cathy was killed, was Wednesday. Church night.

"Another reason for the increase is the improved highway system. It's easy nowadays to bring in a big eighteen-wheeler, fill it with grain and zip to a neighboring state via the interstate."

"Grain?" Peter looked about to laugh.

"You bet. Your stereo might have your social security number stamped on it, so it can be traced if stolen, but how do you put an ID number on grain or milk? Livestock, when slaughtered and skinned doesn't have any brands or tags either, although some farmers are experimenting with implanting microchips to brand their animals. By and large though, produce rustling is not that hard. Even trees can be rustled if you put a big enough muffler on your chainsaw."

The students laughed. "So how come we don't see Clint Eastwood chasing tree rustlers in the movies?" said Marie.

"I think Hollywood has missed the perfect plot," Dr. K said.

"But surely there's less murder in the country than in the cities," said Jenny.

"No, there's more. I mean, there are fewer people, so there are fewer actual murders, but on a per capita basis there are more, again for similar reasons. One . . ."

Uh-oh, he's numbering points, Molly smiled to herself; he's in full professor mode now. But she could see the students were fascinated.

Dr. K thought for a minute, again dredging through mental files. "One, the fragmentation of communities I talked about just now makes it easier to give in to a murderous impulse. Two, the prevalence of guns. Every household has them, even mine, although they tend to be hunting weapons rather than handguns."

"Every farmer hunts," said Marie, clearly disapproving.

"Not necessarily, but every farmer has to deal with varmits—rabid skunks or raccoons, groundhogs in a grain bin, rattlesnakes. No, a gun is a necessity in the country, but their commonness makes murder easier.

"Three, medical services are poorer in rural areas so what might be a gunshot wound and just felonious assault in a city with a trauma center is more likely to be murder in the country.

"And four, opportunity—there's no place to go when you're home. You can't run to a mall or a movie to cool down after a quarrel, so your obnoxious family is always around, and with no community to help talk you out of it, bang. Most victims not only know their killers, but are related to them.

"So the image you suburban types have—are most of you from suburbs?" Heads nodded all around. "Cleveland?" Several more nods. "Cincinnati?" More nods. "Columbus?" A few more nods. "Where else?"

"Pittsburgh."

"Chicago."

"Really?" said Dr. K, distracted now. "We're from Chicago; what part?"

"Oak Park."

"Jefferson Park, for us." The student nodded with an I'm not sure where that is, but I'm a native so I must pretend I do expression on her face.

"Anyway, that image we suburbanites have of happy country folk who don't lock their doors at night is completely false. Truth is, in survey after survey, rural people are more frightened of crime than people in other regions."

"Maybe we should do a survey of crime in this area," Peter said.

Oh no, Molly thought; John will never believe I didn't put them up to it.

"How will that serve the people? This is to be a service project, not just a research project," Dr. K asked.

"I know," Jenny said. "Let's organize a neighborhood watch program. We'll need the survey to convince people they need a watch."

"People live so far apart or surrounded by such dense woods they often can't see one another's houses," Dr. K advised.

"Then we'll make it a telephone watch—with people responsible for calling each other every so often—that could help if people are ill or have car trouble too."

"But—" Dr. K stopped, then switched tone abruptly. "Well, then, what do the rest of you think of that?"

The rest thought it was great.

8

SUSPECTS

The students broke into small groups and began poring over the three county maps Dr. K had set out. Within an hour they'd organized committees for each region. The chatter level was high and growing when Molly heard a pickup pull in. It was Matins.

"So you're having the loud party after all," he shouted when she stepped on the porch.

"No, I'm organizing the rural crime study."

"You evil woman. Betty sent me over with these." He got out of the truck and pulled three cantaloupes from the front seat.

"They're beautiful. How goes your day?"

"Not so good. No good suspects."

"You were so sure this morning."

"That was then; this is now."

"Any idea why she was killed?"

"Molly, if I knew that, I'd have suspects."

"How are you investigating it? Aren't both your deputies away moving furniture somewhere?"

"Yep. We got a deal with Columbus. They send down one of their nail clipper teams when we need it."

"Nail clippers?"

"Forensics. The guys obsessed with nanograms of hair and microns of blood and scrapings and dustings and nonsense like that."

"I take it you're not enthusiastic about modern scientific detective methods."

"I'm not much enthusiastic about modern illogical detective methods."

"Illogical?"

"I was up all night because those idiots insisted on gathering grain dust samples from a grain mill storeroom, for chrissakes. They bagged up stray feathers; the Mill *sells* chickens. So what's the point? And fingerprints? Fingerprints from any retail business are pointless. Everybody from eighteen counties around who has animals has been in that storeroom. Blood samples, okay. Bullets for sure. But the rest of it was a waste of time and now I have to wait a week or two while their excellencies dillydally getting a report to me. Meanwhile a killer is here among us. Or fleeing."

"Is there anything you can do?"

"Talk to people. Only I'm having a tough time coming up with ideas for who to talk to. I'm looking at Bill Winthrop. He was the last to see her alive, as well as the first to see her dead."

"He saw her?"

"She was alive when he left at four, he said. And dead by eight."

"What motive could Bill possibly have?"

Matins frowned at her. "Molly, I'm not a big believer in motive. I just go for who, not why. Who knows why a person kills? Bill was there. Bill could have done it."

"Paper said she was shot."

"Yeah, shotgun, which means just about anybody in *sixty*

counties could have done it. That's my main reason for *not* suspecting Bill. He spends all his money on guitars. He may be the only man in the county who doesn't own a gun. Still, don't have to own one to use one."

"Any other suspects?"

"Except for Bill, there's only Dave. I, of course, haven't told you this—or anything."

"Understood. Did Dave have an alibi?"

"He said he was home watching TV. I asked what shows and he was able to name most of them, including plots—even some commercials."

"Sounds convincing. You say he couldn't remember them all?"

"Yeah."

"Don't you think someone guilty would have too good a memory for details?"

"Maybe, but I still think he could have taped the evening and watched afterwards."

"Dave wouldn't watch taped commercials."

"Molly, c'mon."

"So. I can't believe it's Dave is all."

"That's for sure. You been by there, haven't you?"

"Yes."

"What'd Dave have to say?"

Molly kept remembering that confession. Embezzlement. Nasty crime. But worth a murder? "Not much. He looked like he hadn't slept at all."

Matins looked at her searchingly. "Have you talked to Louella today?"

"What? Louella? Why?" Molly was startled by the change in subject.

"Just have you talked to her today?"

"What could Louella have to do with it?"

"She's ex-officio head of the Tricounty Old Lady Network, a communications system faster'n the Internet, more thorough than the FBI and tougher than the CIA. Have you talked to her?"

"Well, yes, of course."

"She have anything interesting to say?"

"She said she's related to Cathy."

Matins laughed. "She thinks she's related to every murder victim in the Tricounty since the French and Indian War. No, not her ancestry—did she say anything else?"

"No, but I think she knows something; she was just too pleased with herself when I left. But what could Louella know that's important to you?"

"Don't sell Louella short," Matins said. "She used to be a county commissioner. I never worked with her. She was out of politics before I got elected, but old Sheriff Miller did. He had a lot of respect for her. She knew everything, from who was sleeping with who to what was what. She's alert and seems to talk to you more than anyone else. Let me know if she says anything interesting."

"You are desperate, then?"

"Desperate's kinda strong."

"Paper said James somebody or other was charged with letting dogs run loose. Sounds pretty desperate to me if you'd stoop to arresting dog owners for nothing at all."

"James Butler?"

"If you're arresting people for that, you're desperate."

"C'mon, Molly, his dog is mean. Why's your damn dog missing the party?" Goldie wagged in response to her alternative name.

"It's not a party; it's a meeting. One of the students was allergic."

"C'mere, you orn'ry thing." Goldie trotted over, amazed at the evening's continuing attention. Matins patted her, ruffling her ears. "Anyone ever tell you you're the prettiest mutt on the ridge?" Matins started to leave.

"Tell Betty thanks for the cantaloupes and tell her I have beans if she wants them," Molly said.

"I will. G'night."

Later as Molly and Ken were preparing for bed she told him of Matins' ideas about Bill and Louella. "Bill does seem a weird sort to me," Molly said. "The way he quits; he's so scrawny; and his hands tremble. I think he's a drug user."

"Maybe," Ken said, "but a drug abuser isn't necessarily a murderer."

"He's a strange man, though."

"Who in the Tricounty isn't? Think of some of the people we know of. Who's that lady who grows poisonous plants?"

"Zenith Wheeler?"

"Yeah, and there's the couple who preach from their Harleys."

"Yes, the Christian Bikers; I don't know their names."

"How about the organic dumpsters?"

Molly laughed. "I love those two, the farmers who have a commercial organic farm on half their land and a private toxic dumpsite on the other."

"Right, the two-income rule, never mind the paradox."

Molly thought a minute. "What about Dave's cousin Steve?"

"Nah, he's just stupid, not strange."

"Butcher Cook?"

"Yes, definitely Butcher."

"He's so gentle, though," Molly said. "Cries when a bug is hurt."

"Louella," Ken said.

"You suspect Louella?"

"I thought we were just listing strange people."

"Yes, Louella's a puzzle. I never realized this before, but when John said Louella talks to me more than anyone I wondered if I could be that woman's best friend."

"A strange friendship, then." Ken replied.

"At least as strange as ours."

"No, stranger; we're ordinary."

"It's ordinary to still be married after twenty-six years?"

"Yes. Plain. Boring. Dull. That's us." Ken laughed. "Nobody could put us on a list of strange people."

"Good. Let's never get interesting."

Lights were out. Goldie curled up on the floor by Molly's side of the bed. "She's chosen you tonight, I see," Ken said.

"I guess she's forgiven me for tossing her out of the meeting. How did it go, by the way? Are you pleased with the project?"

"Yes."

"Why did you hesitate when that girl first suggested it?"

He sighed. "I guess after all these years it's good I can still be surprised by their naiveté. These kids lead such privileged lives. Here they were suggesting a telephone network when some people here not only can't afford phones, they're so poor they live in houses that don't have floors. Dirt floors—these kids have never seen such a thing. They can't imagine such a thing. I started to tell them a phone network couldn't be built and then decided that's exactly what I want them to learn. Maybe these projects don't have much impact on problems here, but they have tremendous impact on students. After seeing a dirt floor, these rich kids will be changed forever."

"For the better?"

"I hope so. I hope so."

"Oh my Lord." Molly sat straight up in bed.

"What."

"Christy."

"What?"

"I forgot to ask Dave about Christy. That poor child. Who's taking care of her? How's she taking this? If Dave has full custody now, is she going to be separated from her little brother? Cathy had a son by someone—she'd not married again, I think— but Christy is so proud of her brother. What about Christy?"

"Molly."

"What?"

"Good night."

FRIDAY

9

THEFTS

Morning again. To-do list again. •Make a list. •Water plants. •Make vet appointment for cat and dog shots. •Find Charlotte Bannich. •Help John find Cathy's killer. Molly pondered that last a moment, then added, "whether he wants my help or not." Wrongbutton's lead story this morning was that City Chicken was missing. City Chicken was a homeless rooster found a few months ago wandering on a street in town. Neighbors started feeding him and he stayed. He roosted at night on Mae Williams' back porch and always did his first crow from the mailbox on the corner of Williams Street and State. But now, Wrongbutton breathlessly reported, City was *gone*.

Molly turned over the slip and reconsidered yesterday's *Far Side* scene. A farmer was approaching a chicken coop with an empty egg basket, thinking, Well, here we go. Three chickens sat on top of the coop with pots of boiling oil ready. The caption said, "Medieval chicken coops."

What is it with chickens lately? Molly thought.

The list continued. •Talk to Louella. •Haircut if time.

•Change sheets.•Cheerios duty. "Cheerios duty" was the family label for "your turn to fix dinner." Dinner duty had been Cheerios duty ever since Todd's interpretation of the chore one night when he was about twelve. He had carefully set the table, including napkin rings and flowers. Then he'd served orange juice, toast, Cheerios and milk.

"This is dinner?" Amanda had shrieked. Fourteen at the time, she never spoke when she could gasp, squeal, shriek or squeak. She had the teenage talent for making a rhetorical question an invitation to a quarrel.

"Todd," Molly said, "why Cheerios?" The parents made both children fix dinner once a week so the kids could learn to take care of themselves.

"Well, you said the menu had to have the four food groups," Todd patiently explained. This was long before the food pyramid. "This has the four groups," he said, pointing them out one by one, "fruit, grain, dairy and protein." He counted the butter as dairy and the milk as protein, then stood waiting for a scolding.

"He's right," Dr. K conceded.

Molly sat down at her place, Ken following, Amanda squawking, "We're not going to eat this?" But they did. Molly worried Todd might keep pulling stunts like that if they didn't stop him, but strangely, after that meal he began to take cooking more seriously, actually reading cookbooks and magazines for menu ideas. He became a much better cook than Amanda.

"I don't understand what's happened here," Molly said to Ken one night after an especially good casserole. She had asked Todd for the recipe, and he'd refused to give it to her, saying it was a professional secret.

"I think for once we did the right thing, by not making an issue of it."

"But why did it work?" Molly asked.

"I don't pretend to understand twelve-year-old boys."

"But you're a guy."

"At his age, I couldn't put a piece of bologna between two slices of white bread, let alone fix a dinner. Or defend the menu."

It was his defense of his stunt that had won her over, Molly now understood. She sometimes wished the Meal Van menus were as thought out. Meals for the Van were a constant challenge. They had to taste good, be low fat, low salt, low calorie, easy to carry and keep warm, varied enough not to bore the clients, and cheap. And they had to suit local tastes, which wasn't easy in a region which was neither North nor South. In southern cooking, grits always came with eggs, tea was always sweet, beans were boiled with ham until they turned gray and a rare steak was brown all the way through. In northern cooking, it was hash browns with eggs, unsweetened tea, steamed beans and a rare steak was pink, a color that made a southerner shudder. But here where so many food traditions had settled, knowing what people would like took some diplomacy. And guesswork.

The hospital helped some with planning, but for the most part she, Patsy and Betty were on their own—with occasional long-distance help from Todd, now in graduate school in chemistry at the University of Chicago. The question What to cook for dinner? was nothing compared to What to cook for the Meal Van?

What to cook for dinner? Molly mused and, inspired by Wrongbutton and *Far Side*, took a chicken out of the freezer. Now where is this Charlotte? she wondered, squinting over last night's county maps. Mrs. Bannich was to be a temporary Van client. She had just had knee surgery, Patsy said, so was hobbling with a walker.

"She'll be all right once she heals, but for now let's add her.

She lives on Hermit Ridge. Do you know that road?" Patsy had said when she'd called.

"Not well."

"You take Dog Holler Road south to Lottsville Run, then go east."

"Which way is that?"

"I'm not sure; is that after the hairpin? If so, right, I think." Molly wondered why she bothered to let Patsy give her directions; she knew she'd use the map anyway and even with the map would still get lost. Twice. Or more. "Okay," Patsy continued, "Lottsville dead-ends on Hermit Ridge, you go right three farms—"

"Farms or trailers?"

"Farms, I think. I don't know. That's what she told me, three farms, and she's on the left."

"You can't miss it, right?" Molly said.

"Right." Patsy laughed.

"I'd better do her last, then," Molly had said.

But now as she studied the map, she changed her mind and decided that even with getting lost several times she'd still do less driving if she did Louella last.

After miles of frustration, she stopped by a promising mailbox, then tried the drive. It climbed straight up to a house on a level rock shelf. A narrow strip of grass was mown around a two-story saltbox. All else around was weeds, brambles or brush. Half a dozen dogs barking furiously surrounded the van when she stopped. Prudently she sat in the van. A heavyset woman with dyed red hair opened the house door and thrust out a four-pronged walker before stepping onto the porch.

"Are you Charlotte Bannich?" Molly shouted over the barking.

"Yes."

"Thank goodness. I'm Molly West, and I'm not lost anymore."

The woman laughed, but still seemed sad in demeanor and dress. I'll try to sit awhile with her, Molly decided. Fellowship; not just food; she repeated Patsy's mantra to herself.

"Those dogs won't bother you; it's safe to get out," Charlotte hollered.

Molly opened the door gingerly to be assaulted by licking.

"Go on, get down," Charlotte shouted. The dogs backed off a little. Molly went to the back to assemble the meal. As always, she took cold dishes from one unit and put them on a tray first. Then she got the hot dishes out, closing the unit quickly to preserve heat. The food still felt warm, but she checked the temperature with her probe to be sure. The dual units in the back, one hot, one cold, were effective, used by pizza companies and caterers all over the country, and could keep meals hot or cold for four hours, but she'd hate to poison a client because she was careless.

"Where would you like to eat this?" Molly said.

"Here's fine," Charlotte said, pointing to the porch rockers.

"Oh good, a rocker. I'll just rest a few minutes while you eat, okay?" Clients sometimes felt uncomfortable eating before someone who wasn't eating, so this was her ruse to sit awhile. It worked, except that Charlotte, barely able to get in and out of a chair, insisted on getting her some iced tea to drink.

Silence.

"So has your family been in this area long?" Molly asked. Questions about ancestors were almost always good conversation starters, she had learned.

"Not long."

"Not long?" Repeating a reply; that would get her talking.

"No, not long."

Um, a tight one, Molly thought, sipping her tea. The dogs panted in a staccato harmony. An uncomfortably quiet staccato harmony.

"Well, I hear you're a champion gardener."

"I've won a few ribbons."

Silence.

More silence.

A locust complained and was answered by another. A mock-ingbird rehearsed a few chirps.

Still silence.

Molly tried again. "Do you keep any animals? Besides those dogs, I mean."

"Just chickens."

"I've always wanted to raise chickens; what kind do you keep?"

"Don't buy from Breyers, then," Charlotte said.

"Really? Why?"

"People just steal them. They want those fancy breeds."

"What?"

"Yes, ma'am. Someone broke into my chicken house last night and took my granddaughter's prize rooster. She was rais-ing that rooster to show at the fair. It was a pretty bird, silver and black and red, with a rose comb and feathered feet. She was real proud of that bird, was raising it fer her 4-H project, now it's too late to get a new one. The poultry show's tomorrow, you know. Poor girl; she's so upset."

Well, Molly thought, ask the right question. The switch from taciturn to voluble had surprised her. "Was that all that was taken, that one bird?"

"That's all."

"Are you sure it wasn't a fox?"

"Yes, Debby, that's my granddaughter, she said she saw a man's tracks by the henhouse when she come over this morn-ing to feed them."

"A man's. Not a child's? Maybe a rival 4-H club member did it?"

"No, Debby said they warn't a kid's."

"Did your dogs bark in the night?"

"Oh, they allus bark. I don't pay it no mind, because it's usually just a deer or skunk or something. Yes, they barked, but I din't think anything of it. Now I wish't I had."

"That's really odd," Molly sympathized.

10

FOOTPRINTS

When Charlotte finished her meal—Salisbury steak, mashed potatoes, southern green beans, fruit cup and roll—she complimented it, Appalachian style, meaning with thinly veiled insult. "That was better than I expected it to be," she'd said. Molly had laughed.

Charlotte then said, "Would you do a small favor for me? I need food for the weekend. I think I can manage if I had a chicken. Would you catch one for me?" Meal Van didn't deliver on weekends, so Charlotte would have to fend for herself until Monday. Molly had never caught a chicken before.

But she couldn't refuse or the woman would go hungry.

"Where's the chicken yard?" she said.

"Over thar." Molly could just see the roof of a small shed through the waist-high weeds. She pushed through them, accompanied by two of the braver dogs, thinking, I do not fear snakes, I do not fear snakes. To ease her nerves she began identifying weeds around her: Johnson grass, goldenrod, fleabane daisy, wild aster, wild millet, jerusalem artichoke.

The chicken yard itself was about the size of her living room, but the ground was bare and dusty. Chickens will do that, she knew, scratch until nothing grows. Gardeners she knew would sometimes build chicken pens over next year's garden; this saved them owning a tiller or buying fertilizer.

Uncertain of herself, she entered the yard and closed the gate behind her. Each chicken eyed her warily, first with one eye, then tilting its head to consider her with the other. There were several dozen, of all colors, red, white and speckled.

Molly first looked for the tracks; Charlotte was right; no kid had made these. They showed regular, not athletic, soles. Any kid would have been wearing Nikes or Reeboks, which would have made patterned treadmarks. These were smooth, with the left tilted, deeper on the left side. The chickens had already scratched some of the detail, but they were still clearly visible.

Molly studied the chickens. Well, here we go, she thought. Good, no boiling oil in sight. Yet.

"Try to get a young one," Charlotte yelled from the porch.

How do you tell? Molly wondered. She approached one bird, which immediately ran past her. She bent for another, which easily fluttered over her head. The birds were so contemptuous of her chasing skills, they didn't bother to squawk. She regrouped, both hands now stretched to either side of her. Then she lunged, plunged, chased, dived and finally had one by a leg. It flapped furiously. She couldn't believe something that small could be so strong.

"Pin its wings," Charlotte coached from the porch.

"How?"

"Just hold them."

Thanks a big bunch, Molly thought. The wings beat against her face; the more she tried to hold the bird the more vigorously it flapped until it escaped and again the chase was on.

"You may as well surrender; I'm not giving up," Molly said to her next target. It glared back. She focused, concentrating her energies on willing that bird to let itself be caught. The bird willed the opposite. Molly darted, left, now right, now forward, the bird outmaneuvering her every time until finally she had it, both hands on its body, pinning the wings. She tucked it under her arm like a football and marched toward the porch, fuming.

"Charlotte," she said with barely restrained fury, "prepare to meet your chicken. Chicken," she growled, "prepare to meet your Maker." And with that she left.

"What happened to you?" Louella gasped when she saw Molly's dusty slacks and disheveled hair.

"I chased a chicken," she said, and told Louella all about it, including the stolen rooster. "Who would do such a strange thing?" Molly wondered.

"I can't say," Louella said, "but I think if you find the rooster thief, you'll find Cathy's killer too."

"Why? That doesn't make sense. What could be the connection?" But once again Louella was through talking for the day.

Later, when Dr. K burst into the kitchen, he sniffed. "Smells great; bread?"

"I made some," Molly said, "but it's quick style, only one rising."

"What's for dinner?" He opened the crock pot. "Chicken cacciatore?"

"I prefer to think of it as chicken catch-it-story," Molly said. He listened, grin broadening, as she told him over dinner about her day.

"I'd give anything to have seen you chase that chicken," he said.

"I'm just glad no one but Charlotte saw it. I was never so glad to get home, open the refrigerator, and see a chicken as God intended—wrapped in polymer."

"What did Matins say about Louella's reaction?"

"I haven't told him. It's ridiculous. How could there be a connection?"

"He did say tell him anything she said."

"You think I should?"

Ken shrugged.

"Maybe you're right. C'mon, Goldie; wanna go? What shall I take over there—ah." She grabbed one of the bread loaves.

11

GAFFS

As Molly approached with Goldie, she could see Betty in her garden, her frown visible all the way to the fence.

"What's the matter?" Molly shouted.

"What am I going to enter in the fair? Nothing looks good enough."

"Your cantaloupes were spectacular."

"But not perfect. You have to find perfect specimens for an entry, and everything is just awful this year."

Molly looked at Betty's garden in disbelief. Not one weed. Only an occasional bug-eaten leaf. Mulch thick and fresh. Everything staked or precisely thinned. Molly's own garden was weed-choked, bug-infested and overgrown.

"Maybe the eggplant," Betty mused.

"My beans are good," Molly said. "Want to borrow some of my beans for the fair?"

"No," Betty said, laughing, "but if you want, I'll enter your beans for you."

"I've never competed before," said Molly.

"It's fun."

"Maybe. What about your tomatoes?"

"Too pink. Blossom ends are spotty."

"Your cukes?"

"Too big."

"Your squash?"

"Too scaly. Too sunburned."

"You're impossible."

"I don't know why I bother. Charlotte Bannich always wins. I think she buys her entries from Kroger's."

"She's not entering this year; no garden because of her knee surgery."

Betty brightened. "How wonderful. I mean, how terrible. That wasn't Christian of me at all. Still." She began looking more intently at her eggplants. "Oh, I'm sorry; Molly, why are you here? Do you want some tea? I'm not being neighborly at all."

"Fairs are important," Molly said. "I'm beginning to appreciate how important."

"Let's get some tea. What are you carrying there? Bread? Happy day."

It sometimes amazed Molly that she and Betty had become friends. Betty was a dyed blonde and tiny, Molly taller and a fiercely undyed graying brunette. Betty had never worked or finished high school; Molly was a college graduate, a professional. In a word, Betty was country; Molly was city. It had taken Betty several years to relax around Molly. Many country women were like that, uncomfortable around city women, Molly had learned.

"They feel they're being judged," Ken had hypothesized when Molly complained once about how unfriendly local women were to her. "I have this study on rural attitudes."

"You always have some study handy," Molly had complained.

"Part of the job. Anyway, this study was done in Maine, but it could as easily have been done here. It discussed the rural inferiority complex, the feeling that if you're so smart why are you here? Rural folk unconsciously assume that if they really had talent they would have left and been a success in the city. So if they stayed, therefore they must be a failure. They feel as if their brains or skills or talents have never really been tested and that you, the city person, don't approve of them because of this."

"So, since I've been a 'success' in the city they're afraid of me?"

"Afraid so."

Gardening brought Molly and Betty together at first. Molly couldn't tell a weed from a sparrow when she started, so her need for Betty's expertise gave Betty the confidence to open up to Molly.

Cooking was another avenue that bound them. When the Meal Van program could afford a part-time cook, Molly suggested Betty. Molly decided with Betty's three children grown, she should try something outside the home. The well-meaning meddling almost destroyed their friendship. Molly kept trying to help Betty and Betty kept letting her. Finally Patsy pulled Molly aside one day and told her bluntly to let Betty figure out how to do her job herself. She'd never have confidence if Molly kept hovering. Betty had been the Meal Van cook for two years now; she still had days when she thought she wasn't meant for a real job. But she also was beginning to have days when she was proud to be a "real working gal" as she put it.

"Is John home?" Molly said as they stepped on the porch. "I've got some thoughts for him."

"Thoughts?" Matins yelled from inside the kitchen.

"Yeah, two," Molly said, stepping inside. Like the garden, the kitchen was perfect. "Why was Cathy at the mill on Wednesday night, church night? Usually, she'd be in church, right?"

"Good question; I should talk to her church folk."

"And the other is something Louella said, but it's really strange."

"So?"

"Did you know about the rooster stolen at Charlotte Bannich's place?"

"No. A theft? It wasn't reported?"

"I didn't ask, but if you don't know about it then I guess it wasn't. Anyway, I told Louella about it, and she said there's a connection, that the rooster thief could be Cathy's killer."

"Damn, I thought we had that stomped out."

"What stomped out?"

"Cockfighting. Thanks, Molly; I'm going to go right now and have a talk with J.B. McKenna."

"The carpenter?"

"No, his daddy."

"Why?"

"I'll explain later."

"If you really think there's a connection, you'd better go look at Charlotte's chicken yard. There's a man's tracks up there, of shoes, not sneakers."

"Really? Molly, you're wonderful," and he started toward his pickup.

She turned to Betty, smiling, pleased at this rare compliment.

"He says I'm wonderful."

Betty shrugged. "Isn't he a jewel?"

"Oh, Molly," Matins said, pausing beside the open truck door, "don't you forget this."

"What?"

"This." He pointed to Goldie. "Yer damn dog."

"So much for me being wonderful," Molly said to Betty.

Betty shrugged again. "So much for him being a jewel."

"Cockfighting?" Molly said, when John had pulled away.

"If roosters are disappearing, mebbe so."

"Then maybe I should have told him about City Chicken's disappearance. That was Wrongbutton's big story this morning."

"I'll tell him for you." Betty looked troubled. "Lord, I hope there's not another game starting up in the county. Those can get real ugly."

"What is cockfighting?"

"My, you are a city gal, aren't you? Umpteen years in the country and you still don't know anything."

"Well, I know this much; it's roosters fighting, but why is John so upset about it?"

Betty's face clouded. "It's personal."

"I'm sorry."

"No, I mean, it's not just sheriffing with him. Half the time when state police raid a pit they find the local sheriff's there. For John, though, cockfighting and gambling aren't a good ol' boy thing, but evil, real evil."

"Why?"

"When we were first married, I was pregnant and he wasn't working, so we were dead broke. He'd get odd jobs, but we was real poor, so one night he went to a cockfight and gambled all we had. He was trying to get money so I could get to a doctor. You couldn't get health care or welfare if you was married."

"Oh."

"And he lost it all. I never did get to a doctor."

"But you were okay; your baby was okay?"

"No, Molly, I nearly died. We lost the baby. For a time we was afraid I couldn't have kids. John's never forgiven himself. He blames himself for losing that baby. I don't. He was trying his best to get money, but gambling's not the way to do it. I think he's trying to protect every wife and child in the county by stomping out those games."

"What's the appeal of them?"

"I think the blood is part of it."

"Blood?" said Molly with a grimace.

"Yes. Cockfights are to the death most of the time."

"Maybe I'm an idiot, but how does a chicken kill another chicken?"

"They put gaffs on their feet. Tiny swords, spurs like."

"Spurs?"

"Uh-huh. Roosters slash with their feet. If two roosters meet up just natural they squawk and kick and peck, but one usually backs up and neither'n gets hurt. But with those gaffs one fer sure gets killed and the other is usually too bloody to keep alive.

The guys must be runnin' out of roosters if they astarting to steal 'em."

"Sounds awful. So they bet on which rooster will win?"

"Bettin's the point."

"Where do they hold these fights?"

Betty took a slow sip of her tea. "Well now, that's the question, ain't it?"

12

Icons

"Dave called; he wants you to call him back," Ken said when Molly and Goldie clattered back into the kitchen. He was sitting on the floor playing with the puppy. "This little guy's looking lots better. Maybe we put him up for adoption in two weeks?"

"He'll be what then? Ten weeks?" she said.

"I guess; hard to tell with abandoned ones like this."

Molly—and Goldie—sat down beside him. At once, the puppy started wrestling with Goldie who, having cared for about a half-dozen foundlings by now, gently wrapped her paws around him in a bear hug and rolled back and forth on her back, pretending to gnaw him. The puppy gnawed in earnest.

"Maybe Puppy Rescue needs to start a chicken rescue division," Molly said.

"What?"

"John thinks a cockfighting ring has started up in the county, Louella thinks it has something to do with Cathy's murder, and Betty has been telling me about cockfights. They're awful. They tie minature swords to the birds' feet to make them bloodier."

"Well, yes, I'll grant they're awful, but there's more to a cockfight than chickens. They're historically significant ethno-graphic icons."

"How sweet. How many women hear words like 'ethno-graphic' while sitting cozily on the floor with their husbands?"

"If you'll remove some clothes, I'll use shorter words."

"Like icons?"

"Did I ever tell you I give a lecture on cockfighting in the Ap-palachian Culture course?"

"No. Why?"

"Because ideas about animals define a culture; they disguise potent or maybe threatening ideas. When animals are wor-shiped or taboo, comic or wise, eaten or pets or used for sport, these ideas hide important cultural feelings."

"But real roosters get slaughtered."

"So do real beef cows for another cultural icon, the Ameri-can hamburger."

"That's not the same."

"It's not? Eating a cow would disgust a Hindu. Native Amer-icans ate dogs; the French eat horsemeat. The idea of eating ei-ther horse or dog disgusts Americans. Egypt worshiped cats. Medieval Europeans slaughtered them as manifestations of the devil. Owls are wise in some cultures, emblems of death in oth-ers. The cockfight is only one of hundreds of ideas about what animals are and are for."

"You talk as if it could be thought of as dispassionately as an Egyptian mummified cat. But it's now and it's cruel and it's il-legal," Molly protested.

"Anything can be talked about dispassionately. Or passion-ately. Pick it. I'm easy."

"Okay. Passion," Molly said.

"I think cockfighting is barbaric and degrading. Now will you take your clothes off?"

"Wait, not here." She laughed. "On second thought, give me the dispassionate version first."

"I'll need to look at my notes; I'm not giving that lecture for weeks. It's an emotional topic for students, so I put it later in the course, after I've built rapport with them."

He stood up so abruptly from the floor that Goldie barked, and walked through the living room to his study. If ever two rooms were opposite, these were. Where the living room was cluttered, colorful, chaotic and textured, the study was spare, neutral, peaceful and smooth. The entry wall was filled with bookshelves from floor to ceiling. Unlike the books in the living room with titles like *The Cartoon History of the Universe*, *The Curse of Madame C*, *Ohio Trivia*, *Field Guide to the Birds*, books in here had titles like *The Poverty Debate*, *Smoky Mountain Voices*, *Appalachia: Social Context Past and Present*. The side walls were bare except for a year planner with weeks of the term marked in red, exams in blue. The wall opposite the bookshelves was all windowed and overlooked the garden, just visible in the deepening twilight. A slab running the length of the wall and supported by three file cabinets served as a table. A computer with printer and modem sat on one end. Two black leather chairs and a braided rug completed the room.

This was where Ken graded his papers, surfed the Internet, prepped his lectures and hid. The room had been their bedroom for many years, but now with Amanda on her own as a graphic designer in Cleveland, they had moved into her room, and Ken, who used to share Molly's sewing room with her, now had this space for his own, except that Molly used the computer for Meal Van accounts. Just walking into his study made him seem calmer, more at ease to her. If I'd known how much he needed this space, she'd thought many times since they'd set it up, I'd have packed away my sewing years ago. Or put it in the living room—who'd notice?

Ken was intently sliding fingers over file labels in one of the cabinets. He paused and pulled out a thick folder. Molly was shocked.

"All that on cockfighting?"

"All that."

"What got you interested?"

"In grad school I had to read an essay by Clifford Geertz on the Balinese cockfight. It's considered a classic ethnographic study—a model of how to get past the outsider syndrome to really understand people. Balinese are notoriously diffident to strangers. The only way—until Geertz—to study them was to be one."

"Sort of like trying to understand Appalachian Ohio," Molly said.

"Or Chicago housing projects." Ken continued, "It's the central problem in any cultural research. Gregory Bateson and Margaret Mead, two pioneers of modern methodology—"

"I know who they are," Molly said.

"Well, they coined the term 'away' to describe native demeanor to the outsider. The locals will talk to you, look at you, but nothing happens. People chop their firewood, carry their baskets, pound their meal, but something is missing, they are just too polite, not here, 'away.' After a while, and if you're lucky, and usually for reasons that almost no one ever understands, you're accepted. Then the locals are seen for what they are, warm, sensitive, complex, sympathetic, energetic, human."

"I think the locals have been away all my years here," Molly said.

"A few accept us though—Dave, John and Betty, and young J. B. does, I think."

"Why do you say so?"

"When he was building that deck for us, he was trying to tell me about a neighbor of his who didn't know how to garden very well and always planted too many tomatoes. J. B.'s phrase was, 'He thinks he's country, but he's not.' I knew the kind of person he meant, but I was even more surprised he thought I'd know. I'd crossed some line with him and he felt he could talk to me. I'd like to know what I did."

"How did—what's his name, Berts?"

"Geertz."

"How did Geertz get past the outsider syndrome?"

"He was at a cockfight and it was raided by a truckful of police with machine guns. So like everybody else, he ran, forgetting he was European and could have just hauled out his identity papers. Not knowing where to go, he followed another man into his yard. The man's wife, apparently practiced at this sort of thing, whipped out some chairs and a teapot. They were all sitting there calmly pretending to sip tea when the police burst in. To Geertz's astonishment his ad-hoc host claimed Geertz had been there all afternoon discussing Balinese culture. He went into great detail about who Geertz was and why he was there and what his credentials were. Geertz didn't even know this man's name yet, like everyone else in town it turned out, he knew all about Geertz.

"The police, very confused, went away, and after that Geertz found that not only was he no longer invisible, but he had to tell his story many times, to everyone's great delight, while others chimed in with embellishments of their own and about how funny he looked diving over a wall or scrambling through the brush. Even the priest, who would never take part in something as immoral as a cockfight, called Geertz in to hear his story, a real coup because the priests almost never talked to Europeans. He believed his acting like them by running is why everyone accepted him."

"Maybe it was doing something illegal together," Molly said.

"Now that's an idea. I'll have to think about that. Anyway, my lecture, 'The Cockfight: A Sociosexual Analysis of Forbidden Desires.' Do you want to hear it?"

"Sex. I knew it."

"No, come on. It's not that it's a sultry Friday night; it's not that you look lovely sitting there draped in two mutts. It's just that anything involving the word 'cock' is going to have sexual connotations. In most languages the slang for rooster is, as in English, rather obscene, or at least masculine. The Balinese word for cock, *sabung*, can also mean 'hero, warrior, champion, tough guy, lady-killer or political candidate.'"

"Political candidate?"

"Fits, doesn't it?"

"Students ought to love this lecture."

"Actually, it makes them uneasy. I've had some walk out."

"Girls?"

"Both—I think most of the walkouts were strongly religious. For them and even for the less devout I have to phrase things carefully. If I don't, they never see beyond the titters to my point, which is that all cultures create symbols for unconscious desires. The taboo is as essential to a culture as the sacred. There could be no sacred, if there were no taboos. Yet both the sacred and taboo are so powerful and so threatening they must be hidden in symbol. This is why social scientists make people uncomfortable; we're always bringing these unconscious things up to a conscious level."

"So the cockfight is a powerful and threatening symbol?"

"A very scary one, yes."

"I don't see it. Disgusting, yes. But taboo? What's taboo about a cockfight?"

"The cockfight, say many scholars who have observed it in many cultures, is a ritual substitution for group male masturbation."

"My God, you don't say that in your lecture?" Molly didn't know whether to be shocked or laugh.

"No, no, no; not so bluntly. Like I said, it's very threatening to people to pull unconscious ideas out of their symbolic disguises."

"And it could get your lights punched out."

"True. No, I just suggest a cockfight has 'potent sexual imagery' and leave it to their imaginations to decide what that means. Plus I use a few well-placed phrases like 'the prefight comparison of cocks,' or 'when a man's cock gets tired,' and when they laugh, as they invariably do, I pretend to be indignant and remind them that I'm discussing birds."

"I'll never see you in this room in quite the same way," Molly said. "I used to think you were here in quiet reflection, and now I know you were just sitting here thinking dirty."

"I didn't think of these things. Here," he said, handing the file to her. "Here are the articles."

She riffled through the thick sheaf. Yes, the titles were sexy: "Gallus as Phallus" was one. "Deep Play" was another.

"What's this?" she said, pulling out a newspaper photograph.

"A friend of mine sent me that from Florida. Authorities found two slum houses, one with an extended family of about thirty living in it, the other, in much better condition, housing the family's fighting cocks."

"Ugh."

"Yes, ugh. I find it curious that the reporter went on and on about the plumbing, but never asked what the cocks meant to the family. It may have been their sole source of income."

"Latin?" Molly said, pulling out another essay.

"Yes. The English translation is in there too. That's an essay by St. Augustine, written in 386 A.D. about a cockfight he watched."

"And they made him a saint?"

Ken laughed. "He was the first scholar to write about them, and his question then is a good one today. He wrote that he understood why cocks fight; it was their God-given nature. The tougher question is why do we like to watch? Is it our God-given nature to be so perverse? That's still a good question today."

"Do you really think the ritual male stuff is why?"

"Not entirely. That's what all those other guys say. There's something to it, but I think there's another dimension, another level to the symbolism in Appalachia that's not found in cock-fighting anywhere else in the world."

"This is *your* idea, now?"

"Yeah. I'd like to do a paper on it too, but I can't. I've never actually been to a cockfight to see for myself."

"What's this deeper level?"

"I think in Appalachia the cockfight is a clan duel."

"I don't understand."

"Okay." He looked at his notes for a few seconds. "We have to remember where people came from who came here and what they found. The first arrivals—"

"Not counting the Wynadot and Shawnee."

"No, sorry, not counting them. The first arivals were poor English, some escaped criminals, some indentured servants breaking their contracts, others whose servitude was legally up. But none were elite. They were unskilled or semiskilled. Few could read or write. That was the late 1600s. The next wave in the 1700s were Irish, Scotch, again not the elite.

"What they found were rugged mountains, impossible for road building or town building, except a few along navigable rivers. Not too many of those either. So while the rest of the country was building towns, hill people were building family clans because the only people you knew or could rely on was your family, or extended family."

"I've never met anyone here who didn't know their family history or who didn't love to talk about it," Molly said.

"Yes, it's deep, this clan feeling. In the extreme isolation here the clan was your community. Its honor became your chief value. This was the infamous 'code of the mountains,' which, simply stated, became 'an insult to my family is an insult to me.' You've heard of the Hatfield-McCoy feud?"

"Of course."

"There were many feuds like that in the eighteenth and nineteen centuries, even some into the twentieth. But the feud is an extreme solution for avenging affronts. Highlanders found other ways to release clan tensions. One of the most popular was the cockfight. Instead of shooting each other, put your cocks in the ring."

Molly giggled.

"Birds. Remember, I'm discussing birds. A cockfight, like the duel, was an *affaire d'honneur*, and like the duel, it has rules."

"Rules?"

"Yes, these fascinate me the most. One universal is that the umpire's decision is final. So great care goes into selecting umpires. Every source I've studied mentions that Abraham Lincoln got his nickname 'Honest Abe' because of the respect men had for the way he officiated at cockfights. The actual fights might last a few minutes or a few seconds, but a bird is in preparation for months and its owner may invest a lifetime of effort into developing bloodlines because his reputation and that of his clan are on the line in the pit. Not to mention his life, if they decide to fight with guns instead of cocks."

"Put that way, cockfights almost sound like the lesser of two evils," Molly said.

"That's how I'm starting to think of them. While the sexual imagery is important, in Applachia the cockfight endures because it's a substitute for the clan war, a less violent, less cruel way of resolving insults. Less cruel to people anyway."

"Taken to extreme, then, the cockfight preserves family values?"

"Whew." Ken laughed. "Glad you're not one of my sophomores. That, like ritual masturbation, might be too threatening a way to say it. But, well, yes. Ironic, isn't it? All politicians defend family values. No politician defends cockfighting."

"A real country paradox."

"Yeah, and like all paradoxes, society can be ingenious in resolving it. For cockfighting there are laws *de jure*—on the books—and laws *de facto*—laws enforced. *De jure*, cockfighting is illegal virtually everywhere. *De facto*, it's everywhere too. No culture has succeeded at stamping it out, perhaps because the release of tension it provides is so necessary."

"Which tension release are you referring to?"

"Guess."

"Something is wrong with all this," Molly said.

"What?"

"I don't know," she said. The file fascinated her. The periodical titles the articles came from were dignified, restrained: *Popular Culture; Psychoanalytic Study of Society; Rural Sociology.* But the contents were so, so what? She could not reconcile their version of cockfighting with Betty's. She kept seeing Betty's face as she'd described her lost child. How long ago did the miscarriage happen? Twenty-five years ago? Thirty years ago? The pain a woman feels for a lost pregnancy endures. Every woman she'd known who'd had one still keenly felt the loss years and years later. Male totems and clan rivalry and ethnowhatever described a great deal. But they couldn't describe what Betty and John had experienced or felt.

At the back of the file was a dog-eared clump of paper. "What's this?" she said.

"That's a copy of *Grit and Steel,* a magazine for cockfighters."

"There's a *magazine* for cockfighters?"

"There're three, *Grit and Steel, Feathered Warrier* and *Gamecock.*"

"Horrors," she said.

Ken laughed.

SATURDAY

13

J.B. III AND IV

Saturday morning was gray and thunderous, perfect for a funeral, rotten for a fair. Patches of fog drifted across the road as Molly drove. She was on her way to Breyers Mill. Dave had asked her for help. When she'd returned his call last night, he'd said he had to try to reopen the Mill. "I have to do business by Monday; I can't afford to stay shut down much longer. Not fair to the employees either. But I'm no good with a computer. Can't hardly turn the thing on. Think you could help me figure out Cathy's system?"

"When?" she'd said.

"Tomorrow, early. Funeral's at ten. And I need to be at the fair by one, so is seven too early? By the way," he'd added with a choked laugh, "I have an opening for business manager if you're interested."

Seven on a Saturday, she'd thought. Then just as rapidly, And alone, at a murder scene, with a suspected murderer. Then ashamed of both thoughts she'd said, "Of course. Meet you there." But she took Goldie with her.

As she pulled into the Mill's gravel lot she saw the yellow

crime-scene tape hanging limply across the porch of one of the smaller buildings. People joked about Matins' bargain tape. It didn't say CRIME SCENE DO NOT ENTER or even CAUTION. It was just plain yellow. Matins, indignant if anyone criticized his cost-saving tape, always insisted most crimes in the county weren't worth the fancier stuff. Now she was grateful for Matins' penny-pinching. The silent ambiguity of the wordless tape was oddly comforting.

Dave hadn't arrived yet, so she waited in the parking lot, leaning against her pickup while Goldie snuffled about. The familiar Mill had an alien feel this morning. Maybe it was the fog; maybe it was her awareness of what had happened here. The business sat by itself on a small spur off the main highway surrounded by sycamore trees. Behind a towering granary, which served as the main building, a stream greeted customers with bubbling insistence, bouncing over stones and washing over a small causeway. A wooden mill race diverted water to turn the giant restored wheel attached to the rear of the granary. Its ancient wooden joints creaked rhythmically day and night during tourist season. When the grinding stone inside was engaged for the amusement of the tourists, its zitherlike hum blending with the wheel's creak was genuine music. The stone was silent now. Only the wheel, accompanied by some mockingbirds, broke the stillness of the mists.

The tourist store with the hummingbird feeders was in this granary, and Molly could see through the window the period costumes the staff had to wear when tending the counter. Neatly draped on Shaker-style pegs were gingham dresses, bonnets and shawls for the girls, and overalls and straw hats for the boys. Molly smiled, thinking of the incongruous Reeboks that would invariably peek out from under those gingham skirts whenever the girls bent over the grindstone to pour corn into the hopper above it.

This water-powered wheel was used only to make cornmeal for tourists. The Mill's livestock feeds, the bulk of its business, were ground with electric machines in two of the four smaller, one-story buildings scattered around the parking lot, and even across the lot Molly could smell the mill houses, a strong, yeasty, pleasant odor of flour and oil and time, endless time.

These buildings were old, too, though not as old as the tower. Each had a porch supported by whitewashed tree boles instead of posts. The floors and exterior siding were wide, rough planks; some looked hewn by hand. The grinding buildings were to the right of the parking lot and granary. One building, to the left of the lot, was a farm and garden store for locals, not tourists. And slightly behind this building was the last building, the murder scene, a storehouse.

Dave pulled in, still looking tired. Right behind him in a six-wheeled pickup—quadruple wheels under the bed for hauling weight—was J.B. McKenna IV.

"J.B.'s going to finish the work Bill left," said Dave.

Molly did not say she was relieved not to be alone with Dave this morning nor did she even think such a cruel thing. A hint of a thought maybe, but an out-and-out thought, no. Dave was not a murderer. Of course not.

"I need to show J.B. what to do. Do you mind?"

"I'll come too. Does Matins know you're doing this? Has he 'released' the site yet?" Molly asked.

"Yeah, I called him last night and he said okay. Sooner I'm rid of reminders, the sooner my customers come back. The sooner I come back too," Dave said.

"What are you saying?" she said.

"Molly, I've never felt so awful about anything in my whole life. I can't sleep. I start—" he hesitated, embarrassed—"I start crying, for God's sake."

J.B. had stood silent, but now he shifted his feet, maybe embarrassed to hear a country man admit to crying or maybe just tired of waiting, but it worked. Dave turned toward the shed, Molly and J.B. following.

"How's your family," Molly asked J.B.

"They're fine; the baby's got two teeth now. Sharon's already wanting another one."

"Tooth?"

J.B. laughed. "No. Baby." J.B. had a great laugh. It rang with a timbre that said "born country." J.B. was Amanda's age. He'd played with Todd when both were little and had even asked Amanda out once or twice. Molly, overprotective as always, had worried about that. J.B. seemed a quiet boy, but—well—his dad was always in jail. To her relief, Amanda hadn't been all that infatuated with J.B., though she did like his trucks. His dad, J.B. III, sporadically fixed cars and trucks for an equally sporadic living, so J.B. IV had the very best wheels that scrounging could provide.

The boy had taken up carpentry in high school, gone on to a local votech school—paying for it himself—and then started working for a contractor up north in Chillicothe. J.B. hadn't liked this job because his boss was a perfectionist, always making the guys do things over until they got it right. This fussiness had taught J.B. a lot, however, and he'd turned into a first-rate carpenter. Six months ago J.B. had started out on his own and was doing well. Shyly he told Molly one day he was thinking now maybe he and Sharon could get married, even though it would mean she'd lose her welfare with its crucial health coverage.

Even if J.B. IV's reputation as a trustworthy young man was growing, it'd have to go some to overshadow the notoriety of his dad. J.B. III was a rowdy. Just about everyone, including the sheriff, was amazed J.B. IV didn't turn out the same. The man's rowdiness kept his family poor. They lived not in a house or trailer but in a trio of fixed-up school buses.

Once, when J.B. IV had been working at the Wests', he'd told Ken his dream was to build his mother a real house. Ken had made what he'd thought were appropriate noises, but to his surprise the young man had become offended.

"No, Dad's got those buses fixed up purty nice," he'd protested, then added, "C'mon, I'll show you."

Ken eagerly hopped in the truck and the two disappeared for a few hours. When they came back, Ken slammed into the house as excited as a kid.

"Molly, Molly, I wish you'd seen it. The place is unbelievable. They've got one bus as bedrooms for the kids. Another bus is the kitchen/dining—"

"Do they have plumbing?" Molly asked.

"Well, yes and no. There's a hand pump in the kitchen which pulls water from a cistern under the bus. And there's a shower cave."

"Cave?"

"Yeah, they've dug a cave into the cliffside behind the buses, put a door on it, put a pit for stones below and solar heated tanks above. They catch rainwater that flows off the cliff in one tank. The solar panels are his own invention, corrugated metal painted black, with glass above. The water is heated as it flows between the glass and metal panels from the upper to lower tank. A set of filters cleans the water as it falls from the cold to the hot tank. The best feature is, they can heat those stones underneath the cave. When the hot water drips on the hot stones they have a steam bath."

"A sauna?" Molly said, impressed. "Better than a hot tub. They have an outhouse?"

"No, an indoor composting toilet. Again, his own invention. Instead of flushing, you dump a load of sawdust or lime down. Outside there's a turn crank on the—what would you call it—receptacle? And space to get a wheelbarrow under. Judging by their vegetable garden, I'd say the compost gets good use. The neatest detail, though, is in the kitchen there's a microwave."

"They have electricity?"

"Again, sort of. He's rigged up a series of gas generators and batteries. There's even a TV in the third bus, which is the master bedroom and a family room. J.B.'s mother served us tea, just as formal as you please, and heated the water in that microwave."

"What's she like?"

"Relaxed. Witty. That's where J.B. gets his laugh. She's built the prettiest flower garden in the triangle formed at the center by the buses. Outside the buses, though, it's an auto graveyard. Appalachian lawn ornaments. I know, I know, that's not a politically correct joke," Ken said.

"From your description, the place sounds like some of those homes our aging back-to-the-lander hippies like to build," Molly said.

"I'm wondering who taught whom here? Did the hippies teach J.B. or did he teach them?" Ken said.

"J.B. IV's so smart, maybe J.B. III figured everything out himself."

"He's poor," Ken said, "yet he's so damned clever he's created this terrific home out of nothing—I asked if I could bring my students by; he said he'd be honored. He's a perfect example of a theme I'm trying to build in the Poverty in America course; I argue that poverty is the ultimate test of human ingenuity."

"A country paradox, isn't he," said Molly.

"Indeed," Ken said. "He's ingenious and yet the man can't keep himself out of jail."

The problem was J.B. III drank and when he was drunk he forgot about working and got into bar fights. Though a poor provider, he did have one major redeeming trait, everyone said. He loved those kids. Besides J.B. IV, he had two daughters. When the children were young, J.B. III could be seen every day playing with them, talking to them, taking them places, teaching them. He'd let them play with his tools when he worked on cars and showed them, the girls too, how to use them. Maybe the kids had Salvation Army clothes and charity-drive toys. But no one could say those kids weren't loved. Perhaps that's why

J.B. IV turned out all right, Molly thought, and then realized J.B. was talking to her.

"My dad's madder'n a springtailed hornet at you, Molly."

"Springtailed hornet?"

"Hopping mad."

"Why?"

"Seems you got the sheriff on his case again."

"Me? How?"

"I don't know. I was over there last night getting some parts for the truck when the sheriff rolls in, talks to Dad awhile. They argued about something."

"About me?"

"Something you said."

"I just told him about a stolen rooster, but I didn't say anything about your dad."

"Aha, roosters. So that's what Dad's been up to." J.B. laughed, that wonderful rollicking laugh. "My dad, he do like to gamble, so I bet those boys have got them another cockpit going somewhar's."

Dave didn't think this conversation was funny. "Is Molly in danger, J.B.?"

"From Dad? Are you kidding? Dad wouldn't hurt his own fleas. I've seen him dead drunk and he still just cuddles Mom and us kids. Mom always said if she had to marry a drunk, thank goodness it was a gentle one. Nah, he's a sweetheart, 'cept for those fights, but he only fights with his buddies."

They'd come to the shed and all three fell silent, each facing what had happened inside.

"How come you called Bill, instead of me?" J.B. said finally. He'd paled to see the chalk figure and the brown stains, darker than the ancient bare planks of the floor.

"I wish I had. Cathy might be alive now. You'd have finished the job and she'd have gone on home or to church or whatever. Or you'd have stayed until you were done and she wouldn't have been alone."

"Dave," Molly said softly, "you're not blaming yourself, are you?"

He was silent.

"Somebody did this thing," Molly continued. "If they were determined enough, they'd have done it no matter what. You can't blame yourself for the act of another."

"Easy to say, Molly. I keep thinking, What if."

"Sanding'll remove the chalk here, but not the stain," J.B. said. "This wood's never been sealed, so that blood soaked in real deep."

"Most of this is supposed to be covered by the new shelving anyway, so it'll be out of sight," Dave said.

"I'm afraid that drywall'll have to be patched. Look," J.B. said. The wall was splattered with shot. "I think most of it I can just push in and patch. Here, looks like they've gouged some out."

"Guess that's what the forensics team took," Dave said.

Molly thought how futile this effort would be, trying to erase the murder. Murder lingered without end here. There was a frame shop on a county road about a mile from her house, and there'd been a murder there in 1931. More than sixty years later no one ever said, "I'm going to the frame shop." They said, "I'm going to the frame shop where that murder was."

Maybe it was the sycamores with their ghostly white trunks; maybe it was the frequent fogs, but ghosts of murder victims stayed around. People here said they saw Chief Cornstalk's ghost all the time. They were matter-of-fact in reporting these sightings, as if of course his ghost would be here. Cornstalk had gone to a fort on the river to protest some of the atrocities and treaty violations of the whites. He warned the soldiers that if they didn't do something about squatters coming into Ohio he couldn't control his warriors any longer. While he was at the fort, the soldiers heard a rumor about a Shawnee raid—in fact it was a British raid—and murdered Cornstalk and his sons.

Their spirits were here, folks said. Soon Cathy would be added to the roster of local restless spirits. Her ghost would become as permanent a part of the Mill as the stains on the floor. Nothing Dave could do would prevent it. She'd scream in the night, folks would be saying before long. She'd whisper in the creak of the wheel or sigh in the splatter of the stream. Folks would believe. And so it would be. The Mill was about to be haunted, no matter how skillfully J.B. patched the drywall.

"Well, J.B., look at it, tell me your guesstimate, and we'll dicker, okay?" Dave said. "C'mon, Molly, computer's in the main building."

"Guesstimate?" J.B. called after them. "Man, I'm a professional. I don't never guess."

"Yeah, right," Dave growled back.

14
TRP

Dave?" Molly said. She'd turned on the computer, an IBM compatible, and was studying its software icons. Goldie had curled up under the desk. "If you don't mind my asking . . ." She stopped.

"Yes?"

"Well, how could someone who can't even turn on a computer possibly be embezzling? These days you need to know spreadsheet software to steal."

Dave grinned slowly, sadly. "The embezzling was Cathy's idea. I wasn't really embezzling. She was channeling money through me into a trust fund for Christy's education. Only she wanted to make it tax free, so she had me steal it."

"That's crazy."

"Yeah, I know. She'd tell me how much to take from the cash drawer. It was always piddling amounts, $50, $200, $150, maybe once or twice a month. What's really crazy is she was my only witness to what I was doing. Without her, it looks like I was stealing from her."

"Weren't you worried about a personal audit?"

"I am now."

"Dave; really."

"Well, I never was all that good with money. That was one of our problems when we were married."

She loaded one of the spreadsheet applications and scrolled through the surprisingly short list of existing files. "Can you tell me what this might be?" she said to Dave.

He studied the screen. "Looks like inventory. Is there a date?"

"Not on the document, but . . ." She called up the file manager and reset the view option to show dates and time. "Says here she worked with the file on June twenty-fifth at six-thirty P.M."

"Yeah. We do inventory about then. We're on a fiscal year with July first as the start."

"There's just grains."

"We do it in sections. Grains. Tools. Seeds. Crockery."

"Crockery?"

"A new line Cathy was trying. Speckled dishes and pottery. Looks real country. Tourists like it."

"No chick inventories?"

"We sell them only in the spring and they'd better all be sold by April or May or they aren't chicks anymore."

"What do you do with unsold ones?"

"I don't know what she did with them."

"Hmm." Molly had changed the OPEN menu to SHOW ALL FILES. Dozens of hidden files now filled the screen.

"There are two files here with a *TRP* extension. Why is that?"

Dave looked at the screen. "I don't know what you're asking," he said.

"Here. See? On the list, every file has a three-letter extension after a period. That's DOS protocol."

"DOS?"

"You are a computer innocent, aren't you? Anyway, three letters, every file. Most times her extensions make sense to me.

LST, those look like vendor lists or customer lists." She opened one.

Dave looked at it. *"Vendors."*

She opened a *BGT* file. *"Budget,"* Dave said.

Molly said, "Each one I've looked at so far is either the name of the software—*Works* files are *WKS* for *Works Spreadsheet* or *WDB* for *Works Database*. Or else they're functional—list, budget, accounts. But *TRP*? What's *TRP?"*

"I don't know; which files are they?"

"Here: *Christy. TRP*; and down here: *Recvd. TRP.*"

She tried the *Recvd* file. "It's just a list of dollar amounts with dates. Do you know what for?"

Dave studied it, shook his head.

"They're small, two, three hundred, some less than a hundred. Could they be the amounts you took out of the drawer for Christy?"

Dave had been straddling a chair, his chin leaning on the chair back, but now he sat up, eyes wide, intent on the screen. "Yes, yes, they do seem to match. So is this a record of my embezzles? Ouch. How to look guilty in one easy printout. A prosecutor gets ahold of that and could I go to jail? For murder?"

"Doesn't look good for our side," Molly said. She checked the date. "Last modification was Wednesday," she said. "My God, Dave, at seven-ten P.M. That means Cathy was still alive less than an hour before Bill found her."

"Was Cathy setting me up, Molly? By keeping that record, I mean?"

"Well, she named it *Received*. To me that means income, not outgo. Judging by her other files, she had a real direct mind, called a thing what it is. If it was your money she'd have named it *Expenses* or *Disbursements* or something like that."

"Or *Embezzles*."

"One or two *z*'s?" Molly smiled. She, too, studied the screen. Date. Amount. Nothing else. "Interesting that the dates are almost all Wednesdays. Maybe this is a record of cash received from someone. Having you take it out of the till was to keep it from showing up in the business. Not slick, not big league, but I think she was having you launder money for her. Still a crime, but not the same crime."

"Thanks, Molly, for that gentle wallop. But why? And from whom?"

"Let's look at the other file," Molly said, clicking on *Christy.TRP*. "Drat. It's locked."

"Locked?"

"Yeah, access only by password." Molly shifted window screens to the operating shell. "I've not worked with this brand of hardware before; they have their own shell over *Windows*." She clicked on various icons. The fifth one on the left side of the screen asked her to IDENTIFY.

"This is it," she said. "If I type a password in here, it should let me access any locked files. Usually you need to do that at start up so I'll just warm boot and—"

"Molly, speak English."

"Any idea what the password could be?" she said, ignoring him.

"No."

"Let's see. Most obvious is Cathy's name. Nope. What's her maiden name?"

"Chalmers."

"Really? Then she *is* related to Louella."

"Sure. Everyone's related to Louella."

"Nope. Chalmers doesn't work either. Christy? Nope. Could *TRP* be a clue to the password? What could *TRP* stand for, Dave?"

"I . . . how . . . Molly, slow down. What are you doing?"

"Okay. Cathy set up a password system. Maybe *TRP* is a mnemonic device to help her remember. Is there anything in your business or accounting system that contains the letters *TRP*?"

"I can't think of anything."

"Other extensions are either a name for software or function. I don't see any software icons with those three letters or even with T in it so functions are our best bet. What sort of functions . . . ?"

She leaned back in her chair, then leaned down to scratch Goldie, then crossed her arms, then leaned on her hand, then scratched Goldie again, then leaned again and then crowed: "I know. I got it." She was very pleased with her cleverness. "Term. Rate. Payment."

"What?" Dave said.

"A great spreadsheet tool is the Term function, which calculates future value at compound interest. You give credit to customers, right?"

"Yes."

"At interest?"

"I assume so."

"Well, Cathy must have used that function a lot for Truth in Lending reports and such or to calculate invoices that were accruing interest, so if we try each of these—Term. Nope. Rate. Nope. Payment. Nope. All three. Nope." Molly tried every way of arranging and rearranging the words she could think of. Nothing.

"We had our mortgage from Tricounty National," Dave offered. "That might be the *TR*, but not the *P.*"

"I'll try that, but why lock a mortgage record?" Again nothing.

"You have any other debts or investments?"

"No. Well, a Keogh, of course."

Molly got up to pace. Goldie jumped up eager to go, too, saw that Molly wasn't going anywhere and lay back down again with a sigh. "Okay, every time I get stuck on *King's Quest* or *MYST*, it's because I'm locked into a false assumption. I have to change my thinking or I can't solve the puzzle. So what assumption here is defeating us?"

"*King's Quest?*" Dave said.

"It's a computer fantasy game."

"You? Molly, you don't seem the type. Well, today's a day for secrets, isn't it?"

"I like the games for the puns."

"Hey, one assumption you've made," Dave said, "is that it's a function."

"True. But what else could it be except a function?"

"Names?"

"But we tried that."

Silence, lots of it.

Molly laughed. "Only we didn't try assuming that *TRP* are initials, did we?"

Dave grabbed the Rolodex and turned to the Ts: "Tabler, Theta Chi fraternity . . ."

"A fraternity?"

"We call them if a customer needs grain delivered; the kids get to make a little cash. Tibbets, Total Tree Care, Turner's. There's bunches more Ts."

"Who are these people?"

"Some are customers, some vendors, some services we use, like Turner's is my motorcycle mechanic."

"This way will take forever. Think. Think. Think. Cathy was very logical. So what sort of person would be a logical choice for a password?"

Dave sat. Molly paced. Goldie panted.

"Dave? Who else knew as much about chickens as Cathy?"

"That's easy. Tom Powers."

"What's his middle initial?"

"How would I know?"

"Does he buy stuff from you?"

"Yeah. Wait. Maybe he's signed something. He always bought on credit." Dave flipped through a stack of receipts stuck on a spindle. "Here, T. R. Powers. Wow. Could *TRP* be Powers?"

"Let's try." Molly tapped in Tom, Thomas, Thomas R., Thomas R. Powers. Nothing. "I sure hope she didn't use whatever the R stands for," she said.

"His mother's family is Rollins," Dave said. "His land is from his mother."

She tried that. Again nothing. Finally she typed just Powers. Powers did it. She was in. The Christy file turned out to be twenty-four pages of spreadsheets, each with a neatly centered heading in caps. The heading was always a person's name such as Bennett Williams, Jake Cory, Dow Brown, Tim and JoJo Chalmers, Porter Wilton-Jones and—Molly gasped. "Dave, look."

The name heading that page was J.B. McKenna III.

"Who are these Chalmers?" Molly asked.

"She had no brothers or sisters, so cousins I think, once or twice removed."

Beneath each centered name was a simple list of anywhere from twelve to twenty additional names. The lists were alphabetized and beside each name was a dollar amount, again small amounts ranging from $50 to occasionally as high as $700.

"Any idea what these lists might be?" Molly said.

"None. Not invoices or credit accounts. These guys, the ones I know, at least, buy stuff now and then, but they're not big customers, not the sort, like Powers, who'd have an account."

"Interesting that Powers' name isn't on any of these lists," Molly said.

"Neither is Bill Winthrop's or mine."

Molly raised an eyebrow. "What do you mean?"

"I'm saying I don't know everyone on those lists, but the ones I do are all good ol' boys."

"What's a good ol' boy?"

"A redneck. I thought you knew that."

"A racist?"

"Further south maybe, not so much here. But they're rowdies and hell raisers, like to brag how mean they are."

"Matins says he suspects J.B. III here of cockfighting. Could these be records of cockfights?"

"Maybe. Dollar amounts are about right for single matches

and the whole list might be the matches of a night."

Molly had come to one of the last pages. This one was different. The heading was *Chicks* and the dollar amounts were enough to make Dave whistle. He stood up and leaned over the desk.

"Ten thousand dollars?" he said. "What was Cathy in to? How's this one set up? By name?"

There were no names, just dates going back about ten months. Not every week was listed, but most were—two columns per week, one with small amounts and the other listing $10,000, $8,000, $7,000, never less than $5,000 a week. "What is this thing?" Molly said.

Dave sat back down. "Is this real money?" he croaked.

"I'd guess what's real are the small amounts, which look to be about ten percent of the big ones. Could single nights be that big?"

"I don't know," Dave said, shaking his head.

The next two pages were a series of letter and number codes arranged in boxes:

BW1h	CX1	DX1	EW1h
CX2:BW1	CX2	DW1h	
CX3:BW1	CX3h		CX3:EW1
			CE5*
			CE5:EW1
CE5:BW1		CE5:DW1	CE9h
CB2*	CX2:CX3	CD7*	
	CC1*	CD8h	
		CD7:CD8	
		CD'3*	
CD3':BW			

"This make any sense to you at all?" Molly said to Dave.

"None whatsoever. Molly, go back to the big bucks page." He looked at it, eyes squinting and frowning. "I can't imagine what this is about. In all the years we've been in business we never had a $10,000 sales week, except for an occasional Christmas."

"So this is all news to you?"

"Good Lord, yes."

"May I copy these files, Dave? I think if Cathy was keeping this information and somebody found out about it, then we have a reason for . . . for . . ."

"For shooting her. And the killer may still be looking for these records. Molly, we'd better both be careful. If these guys are the sort Cathy was mixed up with, they're rough. Don't take risks."

"I won't keep the copy. I'll give it right to Matins. I'll need a diskette."

Dave started to reach for one in a case on the desk.

"Wait. Don't touch that," Molly said.

"Why?"

"Well, let's assume the killer didn't have much computer sophistication either. She had all these files hidden so they don't show up on the opening menu. He might have taken a disk from that box thinking that's the only place they were stored. Fingerprints on that disk holder might be useful. Does it look like any disks are missing?"

"I wouldn't know."

"Okay, don't touch it until I've talked to Matins. Any other place where there might be blank disks?"

"Bottom drawer."

Molly found one and started copying files.

"What I can't figure," Dave said, "is why she used Powers' name as the password."

"Are you . . . ?" Molly balked at this question too, but, well, this was a day for secrets. "Are you the father of her son, Dave?"

"No. No. Most definitely not."

"Is Powers?"

"Holy sweet Jesus, I never thought. You know, Molly, I never knew her. She was my wife and my partner and I never guessed any of this."

"What was she like, Dave?"

"She'd been abused as a child. An uncle. He's dead now, the bastard. It made her afraid of so many things. Of people. Of being out in public. Of being poor. I think that's what attracted me to her, she was so vulnerable, so in need of protection. Only nothing could protect her. She was too inside herself, too afraid."

"If she were that shy, how did she manage something as public as fair judging?"

"It wasn't easy for her. She'd be sick to her stomach for days before. What got her through it was the kids who competed. She was crazy about kids. She was a good mother for Christy and Stevie."

"Stevie's the boy?"

Dave nodded.

"How do you feel about him?"

"I understand things now. With Cathy being so abused and all as a girl, she just didn't have normal feelings, all numb inside. She didn't know how things she did affected others. She was carrying on an affair, that was the real issue in our divorce. I saw a counselor after we split and he had some fancy term for Cathy's fear of everything."

"Agoraphobia?"

"That's it. It meant she was afraid of just about everything. He said she also did things without being able to empathize or know how another person would feel. She really didn't grasp why I was hurt by her. She just did things. Stevie is one of those things she just did. I can't blame him for her. I'll adopt him if her family will let me. Christy will come to me by right, but Stevie I may have to fight for."

"Did she leave a will?"

"No, but the partnership agreement gives me right of survivorship. If the family has any sense they'll let me adopt Stevie so he'll inherit the Mill too along with Christy."

"I never suspected any of this," Molly said.

"What did you think of her, Molly?"

"I thought she didn't like me because she was so abrupt whenever we spoke. I never imagined she might be an agoraphobe."

"I think she was more in awe of you than anything, educated as you are. All this, her money and computer skills, were self taught. She was smart, but feared what a trained professional might think of her. I do know this, she'd be real upset to know how easily you figured out her secrets."

"Easy? This was not easy. This is a subtle system. I think the only reason I figured it out is I'm from Chicago. We're born with a natural understanding of the criminal mind."

"You really think she was a criminal?"

Molly shrugged.

J.B. stuck his head in the door. "Ready to dicker?" he said.

"I'll just finish here and leave," Molly said. "I'll see you at the funeral."

"Right," Dave said. He looked shaken.

THESE PEOPLE

The women were dressed up, the men wore jeans. That was the first thing Molly noticed as mourners began drifting in. Ken was, so far, the only man in a suit. She was relieved he'd agreed to come. He could get stubborn when it came to social duties, but this time he didn't complain about having to go to a funeral, although as she looked at his face now and saw its intense concentration, she realized he was "studying an Appalachian funeral," not "paying respects to the deceased."

"Sociologists," she muttered.

"What?" Ken said.

"Stop gawking," she hissed.

"I'm surprised there are so few children," he said.

"Why?"

"My research says these people usually bring their children."

" 'These people?' These people are your friends and neighbors and they happen to live in the twentieth century."

"Maybe that's it. Appalachian culture is disappearing, even if its poverty isn't."

All did look as normal as a funeral anywhere else—though

its being held in the back of a hardware store had confused her for a moment. They'd had to walk through an aisle of bulk nails and paintbrushes to get to the viewing room. The store was open, although one corner of it was draped with a tarp. CLOCKS AND MIRRORS, the sign above the tarp said. She vaguely remembered there was some country superstition about clocks and mirrors and death. As she glanced around the store she saw that every customer was obviously about to be a mourner at the funeral too.

The room in back turned out to be a quite elegant, richly furnished viewing room, with lush carpet, overstuffed sofas and chairs, velvet drapes and appropriate portraits of Jesus and the angels. In front, the casket was open, surrounded by flowers. They had put a blue dress, blue earrings and a white neck scarf on Cathy. Molly could guess why the scarf was needed. Cathy's long blond hair had been arranged to cover her shoulders.

After a moment of silence at the casket, Molly and Ken had sat down together in one of the chair rows. This is when she had rebuked Ken for staring.

"Whatever I'm hoping to see probably disappeared before we were born anyway," he mused "though the authentic location is a nice touch."

"In a hardware store?"

"Yeah, most funeral parlors in rural areas started as sidelines to carpentry, hardware, harness or furniture businesses. Carpenters might have embalming rooms in the back of shops. Hardware stores might stock a few coffins. But dual businesses were typical everywhere. Not unique to Appalachia at all, except it's rare anymore. This must be one of the few old-time combination parlors left anywhere. Wonder how much hardware he sells on funeral days."

"Ken, really. You're awful," Molly said.

"What're you two whisperin' about?" They turned around. Louella.

"Louella, do you know my husband?" Molly said.

Ken rose, eyes twinkling. He'd wanted to meet this particular legend for months now, ever since Molly had started talking about her.

"Don't b'lieve I've ha' the pleasure," Louella said, settling into a chair beside them. She looked ready to hold court. And Ken looked ready to be courtly.

"We were just discussing old-time funerals," Ken said. "Molly thinks there's no such thing as an Appalachian funeral."

"Yes thar is," Louella said. "Dependin' on the family though. Some folks gettin' a bit too uppity nowadays fer proper country buryin'."

"So how's this one so far," Ken said, "proper or improper?"

"Oh, improper. Hits goin' to be disappointin' fer you, fer me, for both 'n us."

"What's so improper, Louella?" Molly said.

"Waal, fer one, hit's heer. Should be at a person's home. I kin remember when they was allus in homes. The embalmer would come to the house, do his stuff, and after, set up the casket in the living room for viewing. When the embalmer was working, everbody ha' t'go outside fer a whiles. We kids would dare one another'n to peek."

"Did you ever?"

"Course I did. Then I had to go and throw up too. Never did that agin. Course I can remember a little before embalming too."

"But Louella, embalming been's accepted ever since President Lincoln's funeral tour. You're too young a lady to remember before that," Ken said. Molly shuddered to herself. Ken was laying it on too thick. Louella would get huffy, she thought, and not talk to him, but no, she melted, charmed by his mushiness.

"Not heer," she said. "Hill folk ha' a horror o' body tampering. Bury 'em quick instead. Some folks kept coffins ready, buy 'em when they's young and use 'em fer storin' grain or tobacco or jist to sit on once't in a whiles."

"Like furniture?"

"Mebbe. I know one feller who wore out three coffins 'fore he used one fer buryin'. Or mebbe too if someone was dying, they start building that coffin afore they's dead. I remember, oh whut was his name, ol' man Snider, yes, ol' Snider was agoin' and they called in the carpenter to build hit. So he was a hammerin' away and Snider pounds his cane. 'Whut's that racket,' he say and they tells him and he yells, 'Quit that, I haint daid yet.' And he got so mad at 'em all, he jist up and lived."

Ken laughed. "What a wonderful story," he said. Then he reached into his jacket and, to Molly's embarrassment, pulled out a notebook. "Would you mind if I took a few notes as we talk?" Molly glared, Ken ignored her. Louella leaned over her cane and smiled, a secret smile. Two other women wandered over to see what was going on. Louella introduced them: Pansy Chalmers, another of Cathy's great aunts and her own cousin twice removed; Bertha Benton Conners Ford, once her sister-in-law and later widow of Jeremy Connors, which made her her brother's sister-in-law and now wife of Pinto Ford, who was—

"Pinto?" Molly said.

"Sh, that's him a'comin over, gets real offended like, if anyone asks about that name."

"Surpris'd the casket's open," Pinto announced, not waiting to be introduced.

"Hush you," his wife Bertha said. "Watch whut you say."

Ken lifted an eyebrow, trying to figure out what taboo was under discussion here. Louella saw the look and with it a chance for mischief too.

"Bertha, now ain't that the first thing you wanted to know, how tore up she was?" Louella said.

"Louella, you shock me," Bertha said.

Louella laughed. "Waal now, warn't it? Warn't you wonderin' whut's under that scarf?"

"Mebbe."

"I like that blue dress," Pansy said, trying to be peacemaker.

Ken wanted to discuss funerals. "But everyone uses embalming around here now, don't they?" he said. "What changed attitudes?"

The women and Pinto exchanged glances. "Moses," they said in unison.

Pansy explained. "Moses Bradley's funeral. I remember it. I was jist a wee thing. Moses Bradley died in July. His great-grandson is where now, Louella?"

"He become a doctor in Ross County."

"Right, anyhow, it was a terrible hot day and that body started to swell and puff and leak juices—and stink, oh my word, I was there. I couldn't hardly breathe. So they moved the funeral outside and the Reverend got going—those days it was proper fer long preaching, warn't it, Louella?"

"Indeed—preacher didn't feel he done his job if he didn't go on until some sinner repented. Sometimes we'd repent jist to get him to hush. Repented once't myself."

"You didn't."

"I did."

"Anyway," Pansy said forcefully, not liking being upstaged, "preacher was going on and on and on and that body exploded."

"I don't believe it," Ken said.

"Lord's truth. Blew up. That shut that Reverend's mouth up. Right quick. Then we buried him hurry up. After that everybody wanted embalming. That's when old Formby got rich enough to build on this fancy parlor."

Young Formby, who looked to be about sixty, was bringing in more flowers just then and had overheard. He grinned.

"The day Moses blowed?" he said.

"Yep."

"People tell that story every funeral."

Ken was rapt. "Tell me more about the preaching," he said.

"Things are too tame nowadays," Pinto said. "Now, Reverend McDaniel's a good man, but he quotes a little Scripture, makes a little lesson and he done. I miss the old style. Preacher warn't no good 'less'n he could make folk cry. Folks talk for days after 'bout was so-'n-so good at gettin' folk to shriek and carry on."

"People cried a lot at funerals?"

"Depends," Louella said. "At the wake we mostly laugh and tol' stories, but at the funeral you supposed to cry. Folks'd discuss it later who carried on the most. To say, 'She took it hard,' was a real nice compliment. I remember when my grandpa died, my grandma threw herself on him and tried to pull him from the box and she kissed him."

"Ugh," Molly said involuntarily.

"Oh, everybody kissed the corpse," Louella said. "I did. 'Kiss Grandpa goodbye,' my mama said. So I did. So cold, though. I never kissed another'n after that, not even my dear Carl."

"Carl?"

"My husband."

"But wakes were happier?" Ken said.

"Agin, depends," Louella said. "Some families be real solemn; some'd be rowdy. Some both."

"I liked the rowdy ones," Pinto said.

Louella continued. "We'd tell jokes and play games and dance. We'd have to stand the corpse up in a corner to make room for the dancing."

Pinto said, "Once we took the corpse out of the box and took turns lyin' in hit. Course we'd been samplin' the likker too."

"I remember we did tongue twisters. And singin'," Pansy said. "Yore sister, Bertha, I remember she ha' sich a pretty voice. Folks allus ast her t' sing."

Bertha Benton Connors Ford nodded. "I met my first husband at a settin' up," she said softly. She had been silently listening until now.

"Frank? Really?" Louella said. "You never tol' me that."

She blushed. Pinto said, "If hit's a good story, tell it, woman. I don't care which husband of your'n it was, long as yore goin' home with me."

Bertha was a shy storyteller, but with Ken and the others prompting she told how she was just fourteen. Her sister had finished singing "Barbara Allen" and gone out to the porch with her sweetheart, her "doney-o" as they used to say then, to do a little courting in the moonlight.

"Lot o' courtin' at settin' ups," Pinto leaned over and whispered to Ken, " 'specially in the haylofts."

Bertha pretended not to have heard. The boy who played banjo for her sister was Frank Benton. He came over and asked if Bertha sang too. They went into the kitchen where some of the other young folk had started a taffy pull and one girl was telling fortunes by reading coffee grounds in a cup.

" 'Read Bertha's,' everyone said. The girl swirled the grounds, looked and then said, 'Your husband is here tonight.'

"I got goosebumps," Bertha said, "and they say I turned white. Then Frank said, 'Read mine,' and he looked real bold right into my eyes. The girl swirled the grinds and they come up jist the same. We both knew right then, though we didn't marry until I was legal age of sixteen."

"Sounds like—'setting ups' you call them instead of 'wakes'?" Ken said.

They nodded.

"Sounds like they were important social events."

"Mebbe the only social events," Louella said.

"They were fun, but funerals warn't," Pansy said, "Leastways for us little kids. I remember jist squirmin' so much my ma sent me outside to play. All that saving grace goin' on. Didn't matter whether hit was a bootlegger or a Christian, you got a river o' words to carry you on to the Hereafter."

"Some preachers never preach for a sinner," Pinto said.

"But some did," Pansy countered. "Nobody die without a sermon."

"I remember somethin' you did once't, Pansy," Louella said.

"Did you two grow up together?" Molly said.

"Oh yes, almost like sisters."

"Whut are you rememberin'?" Pansy said. "I bet hit's somethin' awful."

"Un-hn. We'd been skeedaddled outside agin and you was tired and wanted to go back in, but first you wanted to wash up yore hands. There was a a big tub of lettuce soakin' in a wash-tub under a tree fer the dinner later and you washed yore hands in that lettuce."

Pansy laughed. "I remember that, too, but I also remember gettin' a switchin' fer it because you snitched."

Both women laughed now, so loudly that others looked. People were beginning to arrive and thicken the room. A woman in black entered. "Cathy's mother," Louella whispered. Behind her was Christy and a small boy. And then Dave. Molly watched the mother as she stood numbly by the casket. She tried to imagine what it would be like to lose a child. An unfathomable loss. I could never recover, she thought. If anything happened to Amanda or Todd, I never would mend. Shortly, the mother came over to greet Louella.

"Cathy had a premonition," the mother said to Louella after they'd exchanged sympathetic greetings. "She felt something awful was about to happen."

Louella patted her hands. "Earth has no sorrow heaven can't heal," she said.

The mother moved on. Other people came to greet Louella. She in turn introduced them to Molly and Ken. "This is Jake Cory," Louella dutifully intoned. "He runs that motocross on the edge of town, races every Friday night, right, Jake?"

"Yes'm. Toughest course in southern Ohio."

"How do," Molly said.

"Tim Chalmers, JoJo Chalmers, the Chalmers brothers as in Chalmers Brothers Tire and Auto."

"How do you do; how do you do."

"This here's Bennett Williams; he's sort of an electrician."

"Sort of? Miz Louella, you wound me."

"How do you do, Mr. Williams," Molly said.

She didn't know any of these people, but she was realizing to her terror that she knew all the names. They'd been on Cathy's lists. The diskette was suddenly heavy in her purse. She wanted to be rid of it. Where was Matins? Was one of these men a murderer? At the funeral? Wasn't that a storybook cliché? A real murderer wouldn't go to his victim's funeral, would he? Where *was* Matins?

"This is Dow Brown," Louella was saying.

When Molly had seen that name on Cathy's lists she had thought Dow as in stocks-and-bonds Dow, but now, seeing the man's flowing beard and plaid flannel shirt, she thought the stocks must be rifle stocks and the bonds unrated. "Dow?" she said.

He smiled, a sweet, boyish grin that made Molly warm to him immediately. "My grandpa was a dowser and he wanted me to follow in his footsteps."

"Did you?"

"Well, sometimes. Can't make a living at it these days. Not enough b'lievers."

"J.B. McKenna III," said Louella, continuing the social roll call.

"We've met," Ken said.

J.B. winked at Molly. "I'm mad at you, y'know," he said.

Then a slim, younger man came forward to pay his respects to Louella. He was handsome compared to the others. Tall, with curly ash brown hair, high, jutting cheekbones, tight jeans and a shirt uncharacteristically not plaid. A genuine dress shirt. He stood out. Molly would have noticed him whether he'd come over or not.

"Porter Wilton-Jones," Louella announced.

Oh no, another name from those lists, Molly thought. Matins, please hurry.

"Pleased to meet you, Mr. Wilton-Jones," she said.

"Call me 'Wrongbutton,' ma'am. Most folks do," he said.

16

Slim

The gray mist had surrendered to a heavy rain, turning the gravel walkways of the fairgrounds into a steely paste. People scurried for cover, including Molly. The Exhibit Hall was filled with damp people milling about the now exhibit-laden tables. A knot of people, clumped at one table, abruptly moved en masse to a new table. They were watching the judge, Molly figured when she saw a tiny, brown-haired woman with clipboard pinch a doughnut, taste, frown, adjust her trifocals and jot something down. The watchers tensed when the woman wrote, but remained quiet. Molly paused by the centerpieces display on her way to the Meal Van booth. Number 427, Louella's, now sported a blue ribbon.

Louella had been right about the funeral. It was a disappointment. No one wailed or fainted, although a few quiet tears were shed, especially when they played Cathy's favorite song, "Lord, Don't Let Me Come Home a Stranger." The song told of the singer's "deepest fear," to come home and not be accepted by her family. Of Cathy's many fears, that one must have been major if Ken was right about family being the first among all values in these people's lives. Molly had asked Reverend Mc-Daniels if Cathy had planned to attend Wednesday services. He'd said she hadn't been at Wednesday services in months and lately had been missing Sundays too.

She had watched Cathy's family with mixed feelings. On the one hand it was as dysfunctional as they come. On the other, it had something her own family didn't, a sense of the generations. She had never known her grandmother, hadn't seen or written her cousins for years. She was close to her brother and sister if calls once a month or so and visits at Christmas defined close. Some families saw less of each other than that, she knew. Families elsewhere didn't stay as connected as they did here.

She was grateful no alcoholism or child abuse was hidden within her family but did she envy these people their closeness? Or did she suspect their clannishness caused the tensions that led to the abuses, substance or otherwise? She didn't know what to think.

Her thoughts strayed to a quarrel she and Ken had just after the funeral. She'd chided him for being ghoulish, for using a real event for mere research.

"When else and how else," he'd retorted. "In all the years we've lived here the only funerals we've been invited to are those of others like us, outsiders, the comfortable middle class. I teach Appalachian Culture but I never get to witness it."

"But these are real people; you were intruding on their privacy."

"Molly, I must. It may seem callous to you, but someone has to ask these questions. This is not a hobby; it's a service."

"How? I thought you were so rude taking notes like that."

He'd gripped the wheel in frustration, then taken a deep breath. "Last spring when I taught Poverty in America I showed the students the film *Roger and Me*. It's a wild and funny and controversial film about the decay of Flint, Michigan, when GM closed about eleven plants up there. It's about how people cope with sudden poverty."

"I know the film."

"Well, my students don't. Every time I show it I'm amazed at what they see and don't see. They're always puzzled why he wears a cap and jeans if he's trying to get an interview with the chairman of GM. 'He should be in a suit,' they say, 'if he really wants an appointment.' 'Why do you suppose he isn't,' I say, 'do you think he's stupid?' They really struggle with that, that the jeans might be a metaphorical device.

"Anyway, there's a scene late in the movie when a woman who raises rabbits kills one for dinner. Clubs it. She's used throughout the film as a metaphor for indomitable spirit in the face of adversity. She's a survivor. Nothing conquers that woman, not GM, not government, not poverty either. But all the students see is her clubbing that rabbit. They always flinch. Cover their faces, groan, look away.

"A few scenes later a man is shot in the street. Really shot. It's made clear in context that the scene is not actors, not put on—but a video of a real murder. The students don't react to this scene at all. They've seen too many pretend murders on television to respond to the real thing. They've never been to a real funeral, never seen real death, never felt real horror at violence. Molly, we are living in a world where people can react to the death of a rabbit but not to that of a human being. Yes, I'll take notes. I wish I could take my whole class to Cathy's funeral, make them take notes too."

That had silenced her and yet now she was thinking, Where was the compassion? Horror needs to be understood, yes, but compassion does too. She kept seeing Christy's face in her mind. Ashen. Taut. The child looked forsaken, with a knowingness no child should have. The agony of a motherless child, this can't be studied or taught, only felt. There are limits for the knowing mind and they stopped at that child's face. But wasn't this typical, always thinking of what she should have said long after she could have said it.

Peter's laugh pulled her out of her reverie. She didn't see him because he too was at the center of a cluster of people.

"The Meal Van booth is this popular?" she said when she'd pushed through the crowd.

"Well, not really," he apologized. "We're using the booth for our crime survey too. People are really interested in filling out the forms. They're upset about Ms. Breyers' murder. Everyone says so. Course I tell them about the Van too, Molly, honest."

"Well, I'm here to relieve you."

"You don't need to. Kids from the class are here, they're circulating the grounds with forms. We'll be here all day and we're using the booth as Command Central, so we might as well take care of it too. Besides, Matins was looking for you."

"He's here?"

"Yeah, he said he got your message and to meet him at the poultry show. Better hurry; it starts at noon."

It was twelve-thirty now. She dashed though the rain again to the pavilion where the judging was in progress.

Powers, standing as tall as his stature allowed, was frowning just like the woman with the clipboard. Must be the regulation judging frown, she thought. He walked slowly back and forth in front of a table set up in the center. Six birds, all but one a rooster—the sixth was a goose—rested panting on the table as the children stroked them. A sign on an easel by the barn door said MIXED POULTRY: NOVICE SHOWMANSHIP. The children had tried to dress in white, Molly noticed, with varying degrees of success. Two wore oversize men's T-shirts, probably borrowed from their fathers. One girl had white shorts and a mostly white top, except for its Hard Rock Cafe logo. A boy had tied a white handkerchief around his neck but otherwise he was in blue jeans and striped top. The other two hadn't tried.

The pavilion was actually a roofed porch attached to the barn and surrounded by a rail fence. Bleachers were to one side. Sawdust covered the ground. Powers silently pointed to one bird. The crowd in the bleachers was too noisy for Molly to hear what he said, but the girl, trembling with nervousness, slowly pulled one wing out for display, just as he'd taught her on Thursday.

Molly scanned the crowd for Matins and saw Butcher Cook instead, standing by the bleachers. He saw her at the same time and hurried over.

"I'm a judge," he announced proudly.

"Are you, Butcher?" Molly said, thinking it was nice of Powers to include Butcher in the fair activities.

"An assisn't judge. I caint talk now," he said earnestly. "I got to help Mr. Powers."

"Okay, Butcher. You get back to work," she said.

As he turned to go back to his post Molly saw his footprints in the sawdust, heavy on the left, with smooth soles. Can't be, she thought. Not Butcher.

Upset, she began arguing with herself: I'm not a trained observer. Thousands of footprints might be similar to those at Charlotte's. Even if they are Butcher's, he might steal, not knowing it was wrong, but he'd never kill. He was always trying to nurse wounded birds and even once an earthworm back to health. Eat a dead animal, yes, kill anything, animal or human, never.

But the track was there.

"Hey, Slim," someone in the bleachers yelled, "How's yer goat?"

"Hey, she's prettier'n yourn." This Slim, as his name implied, was gaunt, wearing baggy jeans, a dusty white T-shirt and the inevitable billed cap, which he removed frequently to slick back dun-colored hair with long, bony fingers.

"Slim, whatcha going to do with those billies?" someone else yelled.

Slim giggled, then pulled on a cigarette, giggled again, coughed. Clearly, Slim was enjoying these jibes.

Slim. Goats. Wrongbutton. Louella. Molly remembered now Louella said Slim—what was his name, yes, Slim Coolis—didn't have any goats. And Slim's name was on some of Cathy's lists.

And this was a poultry show, not a goat show. She scanned the bleachers. Some of the men she'd met at the funeral were there now. No Dave. No Matins, either. Where was he? She felt nervous, as if the diskette in her purse were glowing through the leather, visibly giving itself away. If the murderer wasn't at the funeral, was he here?

Powers had picked one of the roosters as winner; the six children filed out. A woman changed the sign: MIXED POULTRY: ADVANCED SHOWMANSHIP. Nine children this time; six roosters, two ducks and a something.

"A guinea hen," Dave said behind her, as if he'd read her mind. She jumped about a foot.

"Whoa." He laughed. "Why so jumpy? Are you okay?"

"Yes, yes. You startled me. What about you? Funerals can be hard work. Are you all right?"

"Yeah."

"You're here sooner than I expected," Molly said.

"I didn't stay long at the house after the graveside service."

"What cemetery?"

"The family one. It's private. On Chalmers Ridge. That's another reason I'm here so soon, the house is right near the graveyard."

"I didn't know there were still family graveyards in use," Molly said.

"Oh, there're quite a few yet, the Rollins clan still use theirs, the Wilton-Joneses do theirs, so do a few other families."

"How'd you get away from the house? My experience of funerals is the gathering at the house afterwards goes on forever," Molly said.

"I nibbled just enough of the food to keep the family from getting mad at me and told them I have business to do here. That's true, actually; I do a lot of selling at this fair."

"Of what?"

"Grain, service, goodwill. Just about every livestock owner in the Tricounty is a customer. Oh, there's someone I need to see—if he doesn't pay his bill soon, I'm going to have to cut him off." Dave went bobbing through the bleacher crowd.

Finally Molly saw Matins. He was standing just inside the barn door watching the crowd. She slipped around behind the bleachers to get to him.

"John, I've got to talk to you somewhere private and maybe somewhere with a computer."

"Is just across the road close enough?" This would be his office, a small square building across the highway from the fairgrounds, which he shared with the Board of Health and the County Extension Service.

In the office Molly took the main chair to operate the computer. John sat, country style, straddling a side chair, just as Dave had done, as she pulled the files up. By the time she clicked on the last page, his face had become flat, impassive. But she knew a storm was behind that look. Quietly he said, "What is going on in this county?"

He grabbed the mouse from Molly and clicked back and forth over the pages of the Christy file. "This is bigger than just a friendly pit, not with those dollar amounts," he said, speaking as much to himself as to Molly. "These here, the ones with $200-$300 amounts, those I'd expect to be normal winnings and losings of a night. Maybe on a really wild night there'd be one or two as high as $2,000 for some matches. But these $10,000 amounts in this Chicks file, that's big-league stuff. Real big. Too big."

"There's more to tell you," Molly said, "Butcher Cook's footprint and Slim Coolis' goat." She told him what she'd seen just now at the poultry show.

"I wish I'd known all this. I was over there watching 'cause I knew if there was a pit going in the county, some of those guys'd be in it, but I'd have been watching even harder if I'd seen these files first. But why a goat hoax?"

"So he doesn't have goats?"

"Nope. What's the connection here?" He sat, still straddling the chair, pulling at his lip. After a time he seemed to reach some conclusion. He said, "Let's print out some of these files. I'll put the diskette in the safe, but let's take the printouts with us."

"Us?"

"Yep."

"We going to talk to Slim?"

"Nope."

"Who then?"

"Louella. But first I want you to do me a little favor."

17

WRONGBUTTON

So, Wrongbutton, how about lending me your logbooks?
No, too blunt.
Mr. Wilton-Jones, do you keep records of your newscasts?
No, still too blunt. Small favor indeed. All Matins wanted was for her to walk up to Wrongbutton where he was broadcasting "live at the fair" and ask him to give her all his notes. Right. No problem.

"If I asked myself," Matins had patiently explained, "he'd immediately be suspicious and invent all sorts of 'station rules' about confidentiality. But if you asked, he'd probably agree easy like."

"But I hardly know him; I just met him for the first time this morning."

"Molly, you could charm the bone out of a pit bull's teeth. Just try."

"But you couldn't use evidence gotten sneakily like this in court, could you?"

"Frankly, I don't care. I don't expect the logs to be evidence.

I just want to see them. Fake news stories are real interesting, don't you think?"

So, here she was, crossing the road back to the fair in rain that had now dwindled to a drizzle. She rehearsed in her mind how she would ask Wrongbutton to let her search his files. She could hear his voice over the public address system as he ballyhooed the station's "remote broadcasting facility," although "facility" might be too ambitious a word for a wobbly card table roofed by a blue plastic tarp overhead and supplied by cardboard boxes of CDs underneath. A rough hand-lettered sign taped to the table promised, "Live from the Fair! It's Tricounty Country. Hits All the Time."

She continued her mental rehearsal.

Say, Porter, may I call you Porter? Could I ravage your office, upend your desk drawers, seize your notes and while I'm at it, bring you some coffee too?

No, too honest. Still the coffee wasn't a bad idea. She stopped at a concession stand, bought two lemon shakeups and stood for a few minutes, watching him work, trying to think how to do this thing. Odd how his on-air voice didn't match his appearance at all. He was much younger and much better looking than his voice. He leaned into the mike as a song ended, and with his unmistakably choppy syntax, misbreathed, "That was Alan Jackson's 'I'm Married to You, Baby, and I Don't Even Know Your Name.' Now here's Trish Yearwood's 'I Want to Go Too Far,' and then next we'll do 'Old Flames Can't Hold a Candle to You' by, gosh, I fergit. I'll tell you later, you jist listen. Or better yet, y'all c'mon down to the fair. Come by and say howdy. Rain's alettin' up."

Ah yes, the ever-professional Wrongbutton. She watched him as he picked up a pencil, wiggled it, tapped it, flipped it, then dropped it. He squirmed in his folding chair, fumbled with CD cases, fiddled with bits of equipment, kicked at the sign. His face was a classic of boredom or perhaps bewilderment, as if he were astonished not to be coping with a crowd of autograph seekers.

At last Molly approached him. "It's too wet and muggy to be broadcasting outdoors," she greeted him.

"That's fer sure. Why, hello agin, Miz West."

"Call me Molly. I brought you a shakeup. You looked like you needed one."

"Thank you." He smiled, surprised and grateful. "Tell the truth I do dread the fair. Too many people. But it's good publicity for the station."

Molly looked again at the noncrowd around them. Right, she thought. Too many people. "How long have you been a broadcaster?" she said, sitting down beside him in a second folding chair.

"In my heart, since I was 'bout ten. Here, working, about three years."

"Is that when folks started calling you Wrongbutton, when you started working at the station?"

He laughed, arms flaying. This knocked a stack of CD holders to the ground. "Oh no, ma'am, I've had that handle since I was three or so. My granma gave it to me 'cause I never could button a shirt right. I had to have some nickname, my dad was a Porter too. What a nickname for an electronics whiz, right?"

A whiz? she thought; perhaps he was joking, but then saw he wasn't. "I thought. . . ."

"The clumsy bit? That's just my on-air persona," Wrongbutton said. He dropped another CD, picked it up, dropped it again, knocking over the mike as he leaned down to the ground to retrieve it. "It's not the real me, but folks remember me and the station because of it," he said. He bumped his head on the table as he grasped the CD. This in turn spilled his shakeup.

"So it's all just an act?" Molly said, grabbing some paper towels from the boxes under the table. They both mopped vigorously to keep the liquid away from the equipment.

"Pretty good, huh?" he said.

"Had me fooled," she said. She righted his cup and poured half of her shakeup into it. "Actually, I like the name Porter Wilton-Jones better. It is quite impressive. You're a junior; your father's named Porter too?"

"More than a junior, Miz, I mean, Molly. The name's been in my family since the first Porter came west in the late 1600s."

"*Sixteen* hundreds?"

"Yeah. About 1690."

"To Ohio?"

"Oh no, this was French and Indian then. We didn't get to Ohio until well after Louella's folks were here. Hers are the oldest here. But the first Wilton-Jones went into the hills of Virginia after his indentured servitude was up."

"An indentured servant?"

"Yeah."

"Why did he choose to come over into service?"

"He warn't no volunteer. He was kidnapped as a boy from London streets. He was maybe five or six years old. That was common then, to steal children and sell them for labor in the Colonies. He was so young he maybe didn't know his last name and maybe not even his first name either. Porter Wilton-Jones's not his name at all. He took the name Porter because that's what he did; he was a porter, tended gate on a Virginia plantation so all he might have ever heard was 'Porter, come here' or 'Porter, do that," so I guess he thought Porter was his name."

"And the Wilton-Jones?"

"That we're not sure; we think it was the name of the man that owned him. When his time was up, they give him a Bible and he went west. He was maybe all of fourteen or fifteen at the time. Came over the mountains with nothing but that Bible."

"Incredible. So which Porter Wilton-Jones are you? Sixth? Seventh?"

"Don't know. We just stopped numbering. I could check the Bible, I guess."

"You still have the Bible?"

"Yes."

"A three-hundred-year-old Bible?"

"Yes, ma'am. It's real fragile. We keep it in a safe deposit box at the bank. My dad showed it to me on my sixteenth birthday. And there at the top, in faded brown ink is the first Porter's name. Course he didn't write it, being he couldn't read or write any. We think maybe his owner wrote for him because the writing says 'Porter o' Wilton Jones' and there's a shaky x beside it, maybe his mark."

"Maybe the owner's wife wrote it," Molly said. "It seems like something a woman, a mother, would do, take pity on a motherless boy."

"It's to think about," said Wrongbutton. "I know I think about him a lot. When I'm down or thinking life's too tough, I think about all he went through. Did he remember his own mother at all? Was he stolen from a happy family or was he a starving orphan on the streets? Maybe he would have starved in London and wouldn't have been alive to forebear me if he warn't kidnapped. Then he had to survive in the wilderness. Nothing but dangers out here when that mark was made. Rattlesnakes, panthers, bears, Shawnee. He had to live in all that. How'd he do all that and him just a boy? I remember how I got all trembly inside when my dad showed me that Bible, all those Porters and my name on there too, the last one—until I have a son."

"You are a fascinating young man, Wrongbutton. My husband would love to talk to you. He teaches Appalachian Culture at the college, you know."

"Does he? I knew he was with the college, didn't know what fer."

"In fact, could I ask a small favor? He's fascinated by your newscasts. They're really local stories. You don't talk about mayhem and politics, but about real people. He would love to study them."

"Really?"

"Indeed yes. Do you keep any kind of record or log of your newscasts?"

"I file each day's notes in a drawer at the studio."

"Could I show them to him?"

"You want to now?"

"Why, yes, is that possible?"

He took out a key. "The studio's in a trailer behind the transmitter on Angel Ridge. File's in my desk."

"I'll bring your key back as soon as I make some copies," Molly said.

She found the studio easily enough once she found the road, but she got lost four times looking for Angel Ridge. The strange thing is, she thought as she turned the key in the studio trailer's lock, I don't even feel guilty for the lies. A year or two more of this and I'll be better than Patsy.

The office was stark, no rug, no curtains. A few posters of country stars, a couple autographed, were taped to the walls. In the desk file drawer in surprisingly neat folders were the day sheets.

Should I snoop any more? she wondered.

Sure she should, she decided. In for a penny, in for a pound. She pulled open all drawers in the desk and cabinet, but found nothing of interest except a very large roll of paper towels. For mopping up those persona spills, no doubt, she thought.

Matins was waiting in his office with a tub of fried chicken and a bag of sides and biscuits when she returned. "I've called Louella and told her she's got company coming for supper."

"Us?"

"Yep. And I called Betty and Ken too. He says to tell you he's sorry; didn't say what for."

"They're joining us?"

"Nope. Just us. Just us chickens."

18

ORN'RY SORTS

The copies of Wrongbutton's day notes were spread on Louella's living room floor. Supper and small talk were finishing up. Louella sat on the couch, Matins in the chair and Molly on the floor. She sifted through the papers, absently listening to their chatter. Outside, the whine of cicadas had been joined by a sudden clatter of clicks. Through the window she saw that a flock of migrating blackbirds had arrived and was settling into Louella's ancient pines for the evening; the clicks were their squabbles for branch space.

Abruptly the flock exploded from the trees and swooped and swirled in dense synchrony before resettling. So many times she had seen that, as many times it had thrilled her. How did they do that, wing to wing, beak to tail, move as one like that? One theory she'd read was that minute subvocalizations or feather twitches sent a signal like a shiver through the flock, creating massive motion with never a collision or injury to individual birds.

The why was no less mystery than the how. A scientist might dryly explain that their graceful unity had evolved as a way to move thousands of birds quickly away from predators or perhaps to teach young birds the migration routes. Molly liked to imagine their swoops were actually minute subvocalizations from God reaffirming that there was underlying order, pattern and harmony, that the relentless evil she saw about her was the illusion, not the reality. Physicists, she had read, sometimes compared particle waves to the flowing of blackbirds, and invisible particles or quanta, they said with ever growing confidence, were the underlying order, pattern or harmony. The twelfth and last particle in quantum theory had just been observed last year, so perhaps it was all true, the universe was order and pattern, but—she finished the thought with a slow smile—the universe began as a messy explosion too. Another one of those country paradoxes, no doubt.

"So fourteen stories here are fake?" Matins said.

"I think so," Louella said. "I don't know everything that goes on in the Tricounty, but this one about Jacob Cory, about his joining the volunteer fire brigade, that's plain funny. You know he was once jailed for arson. He war jist a boy—been a good man since, but people still call him Hotfoot Cory, sometimes to his face."

Matins laughed. "I didn't know that."

"Well, Johnny, how would you; you'd a been three or four when he went to jail."

"Johnny?" Molly said, a glint in her eye.

"She's known me since I was in diapers."

"Changed a few too."

"She can call me Johnny, but nobody else had better try," he growled at Molly. He'd seen the look in her eye.

Louella ignored them. "This story here about J.B. III buying a new air compressor, I doubt much it's true," she said. "He might salvage an old one, but buy new, I don't think so."

"What do you think, Molly?"

"There's got to be some underlying order, some pattern to the fake stories. I don't see it yet, though." Molly spread Cathy's lists beside the day notes. "Why are these names sometimes a heading and other times just a name down on the list?"

Matins said, "Maybe when a name's a heading it's a 'where' and when it's below it's a 'who.' So this list with Cory's name at top, maybe they met at his place that night and these names below are what people won."

"I'm not so sure it's winnings," Molly said.

"What do you mean?" Matins said.

"Dave said Cathy was a self-taught bookkeeper, so maybe she didn't know how to do double entry and show negative balances. Maybe what's recorded here are people's losses."

"Interesting possibility."

Molly pulled out a calculator. "The numbers on the Jacob Cory list total $3,075. Is there? Yes, there is. There's one entry here on the *Chicks* list for the same amount."

She added the Bennett Williams list. "Yeah, it equals another one of the entries on the *Chicks*. But I don't see any of these lists that could equal $10,000."

"For money like that they'd have to go to Kentucky. No pits around here that big," Matins said.

"If so, she'd keep those records somewhere else, if I'm right about how her mind worked," Molly said, "maybe under another password."

"If'n all these guys are losing that much, one of 'em might be mad enough to kill," Louella said.

"Lots of suspects now, yes?" Molly said.

"Lot's of orn'ry sorts fer sure," Louella said.

"Well, let's not jump to conclusions, let's just say maybe we want to talk to some of these guys," Matins said.

"Curiouser and curiouser," Molly said. She was still plying the calculator.

"Now what?"

"Well, the smaller column on the *Chicks* list is clearly ten percent of the bigger amounts. But the amounts on the *Received* list, the ones that Dave was laundering, don't come close to the amounts on *Chicks*."

"Meaning?" Matins said.

"Meaning—now, Cathy's record system is pretty idiosyncratic—but I'm guessing that *Chicks* is a record of what somebody owed Cathy, the deal being she was suppose to get ten percent. *Received* might be a record of what she actually got. So whoever owed her was way behind on payments."

"Meaning Cathy was probably real mad at someone for not keeping his end of the bargain," Matins said.

"If Cathy threatened him, he might of kilt her," Louella said.

"Are you sure Dave didn't know anything about this?" Matins said.

"Unless he's a fine actor," Molly said. "He was too surprised and upset and he didn't try to deny the connection between the *Received* list and his embezzlements. I think Cathy was using him."

"So who'da owed Cathy sich money?" Louella said.

"Let's go back to the where theory," Matins said. "See if we can make sense of that."

Molly leaned back, trying to think. As her concentration deepened, she absently fingered one of Louella's crocheted table scarves. "Is there a fake story about Bennett Williams?" she asked.

"Yes; says he going to Columbus for a Rotary," Louella said.

"I don't know him," Matins said.

"I don't know him well," Louella said, "but he's no businessman; he's kinda rough, a day laborer. Can't imagine him in a suit for Rotary; mebbe he don't even own a suit."

"What about one on Porter Wilton-Jones?" Molly said.

"Now that's real strange," Louella said. "Everybody know him as Wrongbutton, but the story only use his given name."

"Maybe he meant his father," Molly said.

"His daddy? I don't think so and that's one sad story," Louella said. "He and some boys were up partying at his father's house and they'd been drinking a bit maybe. Anyway one of the boys, they were one of the Powers boys, shoved Wrongbutton, and he got mad and shoved back, and his father come out to cool things down and one of those Powers boys—which one was it, Johnny?"

"Not Tom, he's the oldest; I think it was Jerome, the middle boy; all three were there that night, though, Tom, Jerome and Billy."

"Well, anyway, Jerome I guess it was got a shotgun from his truck and he was, even Wrongbutton said so at the trial, just talking tough, he didn't mean to shoot it off, but it went off anyway and it hit Wrongbutton's dad. Paralyzed him. He's in a nursing home now. Jerome went to jail for about a year, but feelings's kinda hard between the Powerses and young Wilton-Jones ever since."

"I talked to Wrongbutton earlier today; he didn't tell me this, but I got the feeling that his father was special to him," said Molly

"That boy's never recovered. Blames himself, I suspect. Nobody'd been hurt if Wrongbutton hadn'ta lost his temper," Louella said.

"What's the fake story say?" Matins asked.

Molly looked at it. "That he's enrolling in barber school at Hocking Tech."

"That's a long ways away," Louella said.

"I doubt he's really going," said Matins, tugging on his lip.

"What's this all about?" Louella said.

"Well, for one thing, Wrongbutton's fake stories are only about people who top Cathy's lists," Molly said, "except for the one about Slim Coolis. Slim isn't used as a heading."

"Yet," said Matins. He kept pulling his lip, his I'm-thinking tug.

Molly separated out the sheets with the false stories and

spread them before her. "Here's something else," she said. "All these day sheets are for a Thursday."

"That *is* something," said Matins.

"And the fake stories are always the second story—yes, there's the pattern, second item on Thursday is the fake," Molly said.

"But why?" said Louella.

"Second on a Thursday. I think it's an announcement, a code, for telling folks where the next fight is going to be," said Matins. "Slim Coolis' place is probably the site of the next one since the fake story was just this Thursday. That's how they're telling people where to go."

"Waal now, that's clever," said Louella. "I'm impressed."

"So we know where, but we don't know when," Matins said.

"It'd be either church time or courtin' time. That's tradition," said Louella.

"What times are those?" said Molly.

Matins said, "Church times would be Wednesday night and Sunday morning."

"Courtin' is o' course Friday and Saturday nights," said Louella.

"Well, it couldn't be Friday nights because that's when Jake Cory's motocross races are, right, Louella?" said Molly. "At the funeral you said so."

"Right, so I did."

Molly added, "I talked to Reverend McDaniel; he said Cathy hadn't been to Wednesday night services in months, and she didn't come often to Sundays anymore either."

"I'm thinking mebbe Wednesdays," said Louella, "because Cathy recorded this money on Wednesdays, right?"

"I'm thinking not; the time is wrong," Matins said. "You've only got that one time, Molly? That seven-ten P.M. Wednesday last?"

"Unfortunately, yes; the system only records the time of the last revision," Molly said.

"If we assume they were always recorded about seven P.M. like this last one, that's too early. Meets would get over about eleven," Matins said. "I'm thinking Wednesdays are when they planned, and they planned at the Mill. Bill Winthrop told me Cathy had insisted he leave for dinner at four. He wasn't done and didn't want to go, but she said she was having a meeting and did he mind. She fixed up for it too, he said. Combed her hair, put on makeup."

"So who do you think she was waiting for?" Molly said.

"Waal, if Wrongbutton did that announcing, ain't things real bad for him?" Louella said.

"Maybe, maybe," Matins said. "And he does have a temper. But he's not on these lists as much as J.B. III. J.B. was real surly with me last night, too surly. Question didn't warrant that much temper. I just asked if he'd heard of a pit starting up, he acted like I'd accused him of murder. Maybe he thought I was."

"J.B. IV says his dad is really gentle, though," Molly said.

"Young J.B. don't know his daddy like I do," Matins replied. "Far as I know he's never hit his wife, but he's threatened people with guns before, vandalized property, beat up people. He can be real mean. And he runs around with women. Cathy might have been fixing up for him."

"My thinkin' is Sunday mornings," said Louella. "Only really big pits do Saturday nights. Little hackers like church times."

"Hackers? I thought those were computer criminals," Molly said.

"We call 'em that ever since I can remember," Louella said. "And that's long before computers was even thought of."

"I think I'm with you, Louella," Matins said. "It's probably Sundays. Big pits can afford to pay bribes and can draw breeders from three states around. Yeah, Sundays it is. Saints in church, sinners in the pits. What do you think, Molly?"

"I think you need to talk to Slim," Molly said.

"I agree. Okay, Molly, I'll take you back to your pickup—"

"No," Louella said, "me and Molly're goin' with you."

"No!" He laughed. "No way."

"Yes! Johnny, you caint barge in here, eat supper wi' me and then dash off wit'out me."

"Begging your pardon, Louella, but I recall I brung that supper with me."

"But you don't know how to get to Slim's and I do."

"I can find it."

"If'n you don't take me, and jist say things ever get to a court, I might not recollect these stories are fakes. And you know you cain't use the day sheets, not the ways you got them."

"You little ol' blackmailer you."

"Johnny, you don't know what it's like being a shut-in, havin' to have other folk rememberin' you, thinkin' to do things for you. I cain't be a pest and allus ask. I'm stuck here unless someone wants me. It's Saturday night and I want to go *out*."

"Well"—Matins smiled and hugged her—"you put it like that, all right, sweetheart, it's a date. Guess it can't hurt if I'm just going to talk to someone. Okay, put on your dancin' cane. We're steppin' out tonight."

SATURDAY
NIGHT

19

STEPPIN' OUT

Louella, almost trembling with excitement, sat, tiny, between Molly and Matins. His lumbering Ford pickup jolted over rutted back roads as the twilight dwindled into night. The sky had cleared and a bright half moon was peeking among the trees. Louella braced against the bumps with her cane. Molly hung on to the door frame. None of them spoke.

Louella's outburst had upset Molly. The loneliness of age and poor health had been stark naked for a second. It had never occurred to Molly before to offer to take any of the Meal Van clients somewhere and she was realizing for the first time that none of them would ever ask. Maybe she should take them places, just to a mall once in a while or a movie, although that would be no small offer. The nearest mall and movie house were way north, all the way to Chillicothe. Her own shopping trips were planned days in advance.

Molly winced as they jolted through a particularly nasty rut. "Louella, you okay?"

"I'm jist perfect," Louella said. Nothing was going to spoil her night out, even extreme discomfort, Molly could see. She smiled to herself. Louella had been giddy as a teenager as she selected what to wear for the evening. Molly went in to help her while Matins waited in the living room, still poring over the printouts and day notes.

Louella, holding up first a blue dress, then a pale gray print, grimaced into the mirror. She seemed to have suddenly dropped a dozen years.

"I like the blue," Molly said.

"Makes me think of poor Cathy's dress."

"The gray is nice," Molly countered.

"Makes me pale as a sycamore." Next Louella examined a green floral print, then the gray again.

"I guess it's the gray," she decided. "The green is too, too . . ."

"Too flashy?" Molly prompted.

"Too something fer sure." Louella primped for twenty minutes, choosing earrings and a necklace, putting on rouge, pinning up her hair in a fresh knot. Molly glanced out into the living room to see if Matins were getting impatient. He wasn't. He sat calmly as if waiting for seventy-something ex–county commissioners to dress were routine sheriffing.

The pickup rounded a hairpin curve and startled a caucus of deer grazing on the grass growing in the road between the wheel ruts. The animals bounded off, white tails flashing, then they paused to look back at the truck. Matins shifted down a gear as the road descended into a hollow.

"Slim's a tad off the beaten track," he said.

"I'm beginning to think he's off any track," Molly said. "Is this still a county road or just a private track?"

"Still county. Well, township actually. They scrape it once or twice."

"A decade?"

"No, a year. Have to scrape it at least once a year to be legally a road to get state money," Matins said.

"If this is a legal road, pot is a legal weed," Molly complained, gasping.

The road had climbed back up the ridge. As Matins crested the hill, he started to turn into a gate and braked sharply.

"We're wrong," he said. "Look."

A score or more of pickups were parked around a lit shed.

"So the pitting's tonight," Louella said. "Waal, surprise, surprise."

Matins backed, sans lights, and parked off the road away from the gate and behind some weeds. Jerusalem artichoke, Molly thought automatically; the tubers are good raw in salads or cooked lightly in stir fries.

"Damn. This is trouble. If I pull away now they'll see us go and if I pull in they'll scatter."

"You're regretting bringing two women, aren't you?" said Molly.

"That, and I wish I was in the cruiser instead of this truck."

"Come in with lights flashing? I thought you didn't want them to see you," Molly said.

"I don't, but the radio's in the cruiser. I'd sure like to call my buddies at state police headquarters for backup. I should get a radio in this truck."

Molly reached into her purse and pulled out a telephone, then laughed at the look on Matins' face. Jaw adraggin', as Louella might say.

"Ken gave it to me," Molly explained. "He didn't like me driving out alone so much on back roads with no way to call for help. I've used it maybe twice."

"For help?"

"No, for fun. To call him both times. It doesn't always work. The hilltops block the signal." She punched the power button. "I'm getting a good signal here, though; you should be able to phone from here." She showed him the controls. Both he and Louella were fascinated and took turns poking at it.

After a time he said, "Wish I could slip this gadget inside that shed there and listen to what's going on."

"Why?"

"Well, I know country folk. If Cathy was part of this little club, they're going to feel she's one of their own and that maybe they have to avenge her. Maybe they think they know who did it and why and will want to take care of this thing all by themselves. Damn, they kept this well hid. I hadn't a clue a pit had started up again. There's never any good comes from them."

Molly saw him for a moment as the young man he once was, desperate to get help for his wife.

"You think they'll really go after the killer on their own?" Molly said.

"An eye for an eye."

"The code of the mountains?" Molly said.

"Yes, it's alive and well in these hollows. And hell on the law."

"When Ken talks about it, he says it's family based, clan based, family against family."

"True; not that simple, though," Matins said. "Hereabouts a family is sometimes more idea than kin. Different branches of a big family might be on different sides of a feud, or unrelated families might link up against another."

"Balkanization," Molly said.

"What?"

"Like Eastern Europe. Feuds there are thousands of years old."

"Well, we're not that old, but we're working on it; some feuds—hard feelings as they're called—are at least a century old. But things have been quiet in the Tricounty for twenty, twenty-five years. Hate to see a clan war start up again."

"War?"

"Yeah, because if someone takes care of it, someone in the opposing family will have to retaliate."

"In this day and age?"

"Yep."

"It's my family and I kin criticize it," Louella said suddenly, "but since Cathy didn't have any brothers, I'd watch the

Chalmers boys. They're just distant cousins, but they are mixed up in this cockfight thing, ain't they?"

"Yeah, I'd like to watch them real close right now, to see who they're mad at."

"You think their enemy might be the killer?" Molly said.

"Their enemy might be who they think is the killer. Big difference. That's what's so tragic about these things. Nine times out of ten the wrong people get killed."

"Well, if I'd a know'd we ware goin' to jist sit here yakking in an ol' truck, I'd of brung my crochet," Louella grumbled.

"I'm willing to ignore a little cockfighting," Matins said, continuing his chain of thought, "but not a clan war. I've got to stop it somehow. Stop it tonight, because it probably is starting tonight."

"Crochet? You crochet?" Molly said. "Did you do all those scarves in your house?"

Louella nodded.

"I've always wanted to learn how to do that," Molly said.

"Why, gal, they's nothin' to it. I kin show you in a sec. You jist get some twine and a hook and I'll teach you."

"Would you? I'd love to make a lacy tablecloth for my dining room."

Matins just looked at them. "I can't believe this," he said. "We're sitting here outside a gathering of some of the or'neriest men in the Tricounty. One of them is probably for sure a killer, the rest are maybe thinking about becomin' killers, and you two're talking about yer knitting."

"Crochet, Johnny, crochet. There's a whole heap o' difference," Louella said.

"You promise now; you'll teach me?" Molly said.

"I promise."

Silence again. An owl called. A family of raccoons rustled in some nearby trees. They could just barely hear the voices and music in the shed.

"I haven't been to a cockfight since my Carl died," Louella said, a strange look in her eye.

"We're not going in there," Matins said. "Don't even think it."

"You used to go to cockfights?" Molly said, shocked.

"Sure did. Caint no one survive on a coal miner's pay. So we'd go and bet. Sometimes we'd take a cock, too, but mostly we'd just bet."

"Women go too?"

"Not a lot, but I did 'cause Carl thought I was good at picking winners."

"You went to these when you were county commissioner?"

"Oh no, I was a proper law abider by then. Besides I didn't get into politics until Carl was gone. Carl never let me work. Men those days felt they warn't men if their wives earned money. I raised a few eggs for cash, but until he died I was jist a housewife. When he was killed, his pension warn't enough to feed kids. I had no job skills, no work history, so I figured that made me a natur'l for politics."

"Carl was killed?"

"Mine accident; happen at Christmas time." Obviously she was going to say nothing more about that.

"Must have been something, a woman running for office."

"It war real unusual. I run first for township commissioner, then county comissioner. I won ever' time because I knew everybody."

"Or knew something about them," Matins commented with a smile.

"That be true."

"And reminded folks about all you knew?" Matins laughed.

"Oh yes, gossip make fer the best campaigns. So, Johnny, think on it. I'm the best gossip here. If you want to know what's going on, you need me in there."

"No, Louella, I can't take you in; they'd not hang around for a friendly gossip if a sheriff walks in."

"You use't to go. Mebbe they'd think you wanted a little gamin'. Not unusual for sheriffs and lawyers and judges and sich to go."

"No; everybody knows how I feel about pits. And why."

"So then you jist stay here. I'll go in like as if Carl war wi' me."

"C'mon, Louella, no one would believe you came alone; everyone knows you need help walking and don't drive anymore."

"Oh, Molly's comin' in wi' me, ain't you, gal?"

Molly's eyes opened wide.

"She know hit's the *only* way I'll agree to teach her crochet," Louella finished.

Molly had typed Ken's exams often enough to have memorized the "eleven cultural traits" that define the hill life: independence, religious fundamentalism, strong family ties, life in harmony with nature, fatalism, traditionalism, honor, fearlessness, allegiance, suspicion of government and knack for trading. A big difference between typing it and seeing it, she was thinking. Here was "independence, fearlessness and born trader" coming from this tiny old woman. And against her was John's version of "honor, traditionalism and allegiance." He was too proud to let anyone, especially a woman, do his work for him, but he couldn't go in there himself because "suspicion of government" was in the way. And "strong family ties" were creating the crisis in the first place.

Louella smiled. She felt she was winning this conflict of values. "I won't stay long an' I won't cause trouble. I'll jist git in, listen a bit, git out."

"Well, if anybody's going to be safe in there it's you. Everybody knows you." Molly was surprised he was weakening, but maybe there was a twelfth trait of hill culture, one Ken didn't know about, namely, "Louella always gets her way."

"Waal, gal, you comin' or ain't you?"

Molly felt her heart sit back in her throat, but for reasons maybe only a sociologist who takes notes at funerals would understand, she said yes.

"Just an hour and then leave, right?" Matins said.

"Right."

"Now I don't care a thing about that pit," he said. "I just want gossip about the murder. The less I know about everything else now, the less I know later, got it?"

"You think I'm an idjit?"

"No, Louella, but you be careful, you hear?"

"Oh, John"—Louella was abruptly a model of ladylike rectitude—"I will need some money."

Reluctantly, he drew out a twenty for her.

"A twenty! Are you daft?"

He shook his head, took out his wallet again and handed her thirty more dollars. "I don't know how I'll explain this expense to the commissioners," he said.

"Whut makes you think I'm to lose it?" Louella said.

20
THE PITS

As the two women opened the shed door, the crowd fell into a stunned silence.

"Hi, boys, I'm joinin' the fun," Louella said.

Slim walked over, frowning. "I'm sorry, Louella, but you ain't welcome here."

"Now, Slim, I was the best cocker in the county before my Carl died. Ask J.B. III over thar. I could pick winners better'n anyone."

"It's true, Slim," J.B. said. "I remember. We'd all try to figure out what she'd bet and she'n Carl'd try to keep it secret so the odds'd be better."

"Well, who's she; she don't belong here," Slim said, pointing to Molly.

"Oh, that's Molly. I promised to teach her to crochet if she'd take me someplace on Saturday night. Course I didn't tell her I wanted to go cockin'."

Taking the cue, Molly did her best aw-shucks grin, and shrugged. It worked; most of the men laughed. J.B. III said, "What'd you think when she brung you here?"

"I thought she was crazy," Molly said, smiling at him, wondering as she did if she had a murderer for an ally. J.B. was the best-dressed man in the shed, by country standards—fancy tooled boots, blue western shirt with mauve piping, faded tight jeans. Though in his fifties, he might have caught Cathy's eye when dressed like that. J.B.'s wife, she noted, was not along.

Slim and a couple of other men discussed things for a minute. "All right, Louella, but Molly stays outside."

Louella brandished her cane and leaned with exaggerated pitifulness on Molly's arm. "I kin hardly stand up and you goin' to take away my helper? Shame on you, Slim. Your momma, rest her soul, raised you to treat folks better'n that."

Uh-oh, Molly thought, tactical error. Momma ploys don't work with grown men. To her surprise Slim growled but stepped aside to let them in. Correction, Molly thought. Momma ploys work with good ol' boys.

The shed, she recognized from her years of back-country driving, was a tobacco barn. Some burley hung in the rafters, but the lower tobacco racks had been set aside to make space for the pit. The pit itself was nothing but bales of hay arranged waist high into a square. A smaller square of bales sat off to one side. Lights were dim but adequate, just a string of naked bulbs strung along the center rafter. A table beside the door had its own gooseneck lamp. A grizzled old man in bib overalls sat at this table, a cash box open in front of him.

"Fee to get in is ten dollars," he said. Molly paid for both of them.

"Who gets these fees?" Molly asked.

"They's split between umpire and host; Slim's host tonight," the man said. Beside him, a boy about fifteen was selling beer and soft drinks from a cooler.

Against the far wall she saw thirty or so cages stacked on tables. A man who looked like a younger version of Slim stood in front of these tables with a stern look on his face. No one came near him or the tables.

The old man saw her glance and said, "It's the host's duty to be sure nobody switches birds in those cages. Slim's got his boy doing the guarding tonight."

Molly smiled at the man, relieved somebody was acting friendly. Louella was anxious to mingle and tugged on her arm. The music, Molly was surprised to see, was live, a trio of banjo, mandolin and fiddle, playing bouncy clogging music. A few men who'd brought wives or dates were dancing. One couple were so good at clogging, others had gathered around to clap rhythm for them. Their torsos rigid, their arms about each other's waist, the two flayed their legs, heel and toe, toe and heel, faster and faster.

The man was just slightly fleshy, not fat, but he wore clothes obviously bought before he'd gained the weight. His jeans were tight, especially in the waist; his tank-style undershirt was taut; and his silver belt buckle, big as Molly's hand, pressed into his belly. He sported a ten-gallon hat and a half-dozen tattoos. His partner was thin with deeply scooped tank top, tight shorts and hair so blond with dye it blazed.

That's what Betty must have looked like when she was young, Molly thought. She suddenly could imagine John here, young, earnest and desperate. There was some of that in the eyes of the young men. She scanned their faces to see whom she recognized. The men from the funeral were all here, she could see, Bennett Williams, Jake Cory, Dow Brown. And Wrongbutton. He stood alone by the smaller hay pit, his forehead furrowed. Sad? she wondered. Worried? He'd changed from his dress shirt of the funeral into regulation country plaid. He was still more handsome than the others, but at least now he was dressed like them. She watched the musicians for a minute; she'd always enjoyed country fiddlers. Bill Winthrop was *not* one of the players. That's worth telling Matins later, she thought.

Most of the crowd milled around two tables beside the larger pit. It was toward these that Louella was dragging Molly. A bird was set on each table. The prefight comparison of cocks, Molly realized and stifled a giggle. Handlers stroked the birds much as the children had at the fair. Would-be bettors who asked to inspect the birds would stretch out the wings, inspect the feet, feel the muscles, check the wattles, again reminding Molly of the fair.

As they approched the tables, Molly saw another face she recognized. Tom Powers stood behind one of the handlers, watching with disapproval the clumsy hands of the bettors. For some minutes now Molly had been overhearing the phrase "the power bird," but she'd thought it was a generic term, something like Mighty Morphin' Power Rangers. Now she understood people had been saying "the Powers bird." One of the birds about to fight belonged to him. He hadn't seen her yet. Had he judged some of these roosters at the fair today? Molly wondered how the children would feel if their roosters didn't come home. Louella pulled her to the Powers table.

No escaping it now; he would see her.

"I see you everywhere," he said, still frowning.

"I guess I go everywhere," Molly said. She noticed a line had been shaved down the bird's spine and part of its tail feathers were trimmed. The lower thighs were shaved too. An electric razor lay on the table, so the shaving must have been done moments ago. To keep the bird from overheating, was Molly's guess as to why.

Louella took the bird from the handler. "A smart bird, is it?" she asked.

"He's a canny fighter," Powers said.

"How canny?"

"Dips instead of rises when attacked."

"Pretty smart." She ran her gnarled hands expertly over the breast and thighs. "Feels right strong. Your line?"

"Been building his line three years. His sire and grandsire were winners. His grandsire died of old age."

"Well now. A bird that good, who'd want to fight him?" Louella said.

Powers smiled for the first time. "You go an' find out yourself, Louella. I'm not goin' to talk up the competition."

"An impressive line," Louella said as they pushed through to the challenger's table. "Someone knows breeding."

Cathy? Molly thought to herself, but said nothing; this was not the place for discussing a murder victim's hobbies.

"Looks like a crossbreed, but can't tell what stock. One of the Asian lines; they make the best fighters," Louella continued.

The challenger was a bigger bird, a white-crested Polish. Again Louella felt the muscles, pinched the feet, stretched the wing. "I don't normally think of these as fighters," she said sharply to the handler.

"Oh, this one is; he be one mean bird," he replied, stroking the bird, which looked more nervous than mean, pushing against his handler for protection.

"Unusual match," Louella said as they left the inspection tables.

"Both birds seem gentle," Molly said.

"Oh, most roosters are. They jist peck other roosters, not people."

Powers and another man were now in earnest conversation. Dow Brown, the occasional dowser, stood by listening.

"Looks like Dow be umpire tonight; good choice. He a good man," Louella said.

The conversation ended, the two men shook hands and Dow stepped into the main pit. This was the signal for the music to stop.

"The bet, ladies and gentlemen, is set. Winner takes $200," Dow called in a singsong voice.

"Small match. Opening match usually is," Louella said. "Now watch the fun as people set their side bets." Louella sat down on a bale and, as at the funeral, waited for people to come to her. J.B. III approached first. Meanwhile, men were calling "Two, two, two" or "Three, three, three." It reminded Molly of the uproar in the pit at the Chicago Board of Trade as sellers and buyers tried to find each other.

"What are they shouting?"

"Odds," Louella said. "Some are offering two, others three to one."

"But on which bird?"

"They's only one way to find out."

"What's that?"

"Bet, silly; go place a bet with one of them."

"No thank you," Molly said. "I'll just watch."

J.B. and Louella fell into deep conversation, whispering into each other's ear. After a few minutes, both pulled out cash from pockets and fanned it, apparently to reassure each other they could cover the bet.

"Now keep it secret, J.B.," Louella said.

He grinned. "They still tell stories about you, Louella; glad you're here. Your secret's safe with me. Besides," he added, now talking to Molly, "if'n I'm good and if'n I lose, she'll tell me next bet what she's betting and I kin recover my losses threefold."

Louella smiled, much like a queen enjoying a triumphal return to her kingdom. Several others approached her and she was busy for a few minutes, again with whispering, showing of cash, promised secrecy.

Louella decided she was done and asked Molly to help her to the pit. People let the women push through to the front. This was the part Molly was dreading. The actual fight. "Why are there two pits?" she asked Louella.

"Fight's not over until one bird dead or quits. Even if a bird is flat on its back, if it still trying to peck, the fight go on, so sometimes they put the tired birds in the small pit to finish and start up another'n in the big pit. Two really game birds can go fer over'n hour. Most fights over in a few minutes, though."

The moment had come. Lights flickered.

"That's the final betting call, not that everyone always re-spects it," Louella said. Two men stepped into the pit. Not own-ers, but handlers, Molly realized—two neutral parties meant to keep the game fair. Two other men followed the handlers.

"Those are the gaffers," Louella said. "They goin' to tie the gaffs to the legs. It's a speciality. Take real skill to do it right."

The spurs. Molly saw to her horror that they were sharp, curved needles, twice as long as a major toe.

"Why do they have to do that?" she said.

"Different birds have different length legs and feet, so the gaffs keep it equal," said Louella.

Molly wanted to argue but again decided this was not the place or time.

The gaffers tested the twine holding the gaffs on their own bird, then each inspected the other bird. Next each handler in-spected the gaffs on both birds and finally the umpire inspected each bird. It had the air of ritual, and Molly wondered how many centuries this had been the custom, first gaffers, then handlers, then umpire. Now the two handlers approached the center; each holding a bird tucked under an arm with wings pinned, much as Molly had done when she'd captured Charlotte's chicken.

Dow nodded at one handler, who held his bird out to let the other bird peck at its neck and wattles. Then they reversed, let-ting the other bird peck at the first one.

"That's so they git the birds mad and wantin' to fight," said Louella.

The watchers roared as at a signal from Dow the handlers tossed the birds toward each other. The two handlers and the umpire leapt back against the bales, moving constantly to keep out of the way of the birds, who now had swelled, puffing up their feathers to look twice as big. They had completely changed from docile table birds to enthusiastic fighters.

The two rose and fell, flapping furiously, stretching, trying to strike. The Polish struck first and hard, its gaff sticking in the

Powers bird. Dow signaled; the two handlers leapt to separate the birds. They carried them to the pit edge, stroked them, splashed them with water and gave them drinks from plastic bottles. Like boxers, Molly thought.

The water in those bottles looked suspiciously cloudy.

"Each trainer has his own secret formula fer whut's in those bottles," Louella said.

"Drugs?" Molly said shocked. "Are drugs legal at cockfights?"

Louella shook her head, wondering how anybody could be so stupid. "Drugs 'bout as legal as these here fights," she said.

Molly laughed at herself. What was she thinking? Rules in this world of course wouldn't match rules in the rest of the world. "Guess I don't have much experience doing illegal things," she told Louella.

Dow signaled the handlers the break was over. The men tossed the birds together again. Now the Powers bird got a nick on the Polish and blood flew all the way to the haystack; then the Polish returned and drew blood too. Molly cringed. Her front-row seat meant not only could she see everything, but she was going to get spattered. The fight wore on, but Molly noticed that Powers was right—when the Polish flew up to attack, the Powers bird ducked.

"That's real rare," Louella said. "Most chickens are too dumb to duck; they just attack and parry. Usually you bet on strength and endurance, not smarts, but Powers may have something here, a real special line."

"Who'd you bet on?"

"I ain't telling."

"Your secret's safe with me, Louella."

"I bet on the Polish."

The Polish had its beak on the Powers bird's wattle; when the bird pulled away, a chunk of its wattle went with the pull. Molly watched the blood gush from the panting bird's neck and decided she needed air. "You going to be okay a few minutes, Louella?" she said. Louella nodded intent on the fray.

She slipped out the door of the shed and breathed, trying to settle her stomach. More men were outside smoking. Well, here's a modern touch, she thought, it's a no-smoking pit. She hadn't noticed until this moment that no one had been smoking inside, and then she wondered if smoking had ever been allowed, since the fights were always held inside flammable hay. Valuable tobacco too could be damaged by smoke, ironically enough.

The smokers hadn't heard her and she realized, her heart freezing, they were talking about Cathy.

"It's got to be an ex-lover what done it," said one voice. "She tended to change her horses a bit. I say she dumped someone and he got mad."

"I say it's an ex-cocker, someone who lost too much money on those birds she and Powers 'a been breeding," said a second voice.

"Do you think she and Powers ever?" a third voice said, leaving the sentence hanging.

"Nah, he's so dumpy and she's so pretty," First Voice said.

"Yeah, but women don't always care about looks. Powers has money. And lots of it. He's been takin' that line into Kentucky and winnin' big in pits down there. None of this hacker stuff for him. Real pits. Big bucks. Not thousand-dollar nights, but ten, twelve grand a night."

"Whew, you sure?"

"No, just I heard."

"Who else might she have, you know, with?"

"You'll laugh," Third Voice said.

"Not Dave again."

"Nah, Dave's a one-at-a-time type; he's got his Barbara now."

"So who? Don't you hold out, you tell me."

"Little ol' Wrongbutton."

"How you know that?"

"I seen 'em."

"Seen 'em?"

"Well, not seen 'em, you know *seen* 'em. But I seen 'em together and they was not unhappy."

"You think he killed her?"

"No. Could be someone killed her 'cause of him. It's the someone before Wrongbutton that's a kilt her, I say."

"And who's that."

"Wrongbutton knows."

"Whew, Wrongbutton's in a wrong place, then, ain't he?"

"Yep. If I was that whoever, I'd be wantin' Wrongbutton gone too."

"Think our clumsy D.J. knows hit?"

"Hope he do."

21

TYFNS

Molly was afraid to move. If she tried to go back inside, the men might hear her or see the light from the doorway. If she stayed where she was, someone would eventually see her and know she'd been listening.

Deciding "naive outsider" was the best disguise, she opened the shed door boldly, slammed it noisily and pretended to just be stepping outside. One of the men poked his head around the corner to see who'd come out.

"Oh, hello," she said. "Stuffy in there. I needed some air."

"Yes; gets close in there." He was cautious.

"Have we met? I'm Molly West. I'm with the Mea—"

"The Meal Van, of course," said one of the others. "Yes, I do know you," relief in his voice. Knowing a person made everything all right. "You helped my granma a couple years ago. We sure did appreciate what you did for her. Without your daily visits we couldn'ta kept her at home and taken care of her. She wanted to die at home and you made it possible. Dyin' at home was real important to her."

"It is to many people, I've learned," she said.

"Ever expected to be at something like this?" another man said; she recognized him as Third Voice, the man who'd "seen" Wrongbutton and Cathy.

"No, most certainly not. I should have known Louella would get me into something bizarre. I'm not the bargainer she is; I never thought to make her tell me where she wanted to go before I agreed." Smooth, she thought; lying like a native, I am.

"You pretty shocked, ain't you?"

"I seem to know you," she said.

"Well, you should. You see me every week. I get your trash."

"Oh, Granger, Scott Granger, yes, hello. Well, this is a relief; I was feeling I didn't know anyone."

"Now, Molly, everybody knows you or Patsy. Slim's a bit fraidy, but you're welcome here."

"Long as you don't talk too much about what you see to your neighbor," one of the others said.

"Dave?"

"No, you silly thing, to Matins."

Now here was a dilemma. How to talk her way through this. Too many people knew who her neighbor was. Well, try Patsy's dictum, the best lie is one that's almost the truth. "Well, tell the truth, I didn't know these were illegal and did tell him I was coming and he said the strangest thing. He said I was not to tell him anything about them because of who he was. He didn't want to have to do anything about them. So I promised. Nothing about the fights."

Of course, anything about the murder, she thought, was different.

"So you pretty shocked by us cockers?"

"Well, my husband, he teaches Appalachian Culture at the college, he's been telling me a few things about these," she said, trying not to smile as she remembered what he'd told her. "They're something different, for sure, but I'll admit I don't understand the appeal."

They laughed.

"Kin you explain, Paul?"

Paul frowned, trying to bring such a complex idea down to her level. "Mostly it's just the gambling and getting together with the fellows. But a real game bird is a thrill to see. The courage, grit, those are good things. I like a bird that's stubborn, won't give up."

"That's how I feel," Scott said. "It's hard making a living in these parts. Everyone struggles. But you see those birds and you know you can go on, keep up the fight."

"But the blood, the death," Molly objected.

"Molly, they're just chickens," Paul said. "A court in Maryland threw out a cockfighting case. Said it couldn't be cruelty; chickens weren't worth the sentiment. Chickens don't even feel pain that much."

"True?"

"I've wrung enough necks to know."

"No; I mean about the court case."

"Yep, just a few years ago too; we got a good laugh out o' that."

Scott picked up the argument. "Even if chickens do feel pain like the Humane types say, that chicken would be in a pot in two months, fighter or no fighter, because they're too tough to eat after about eight months old. Even if it's selected as a breeder, it'd still die of old age at three years. Might as well let them fight, they like it so much."

Paul took his turn at the debate. "This is true; it's their nature to fight. Rooster see another, he always try to beat it off. Every rooster wants t'be cock o' the walk. A pit just lets them do what they want to do anyways."

"But why the spurs?"

"That makes it more fair."

"Fair?" she cried, unable to keep her disgust hidden any longer.

"Sure, birds have different-shaped feet, beaks, heights, so the spurs makes them fight on level ground."

"You think, like boxers, they could separate them by weight."

"They do; anyone with sense sets a match by weight, sometimes to the half ounce."

So why were the birds in this first match mismatched by weight? Molly thought, a suspicion forming in her mind.

"Who decides which bird fights which?" she asked.

"The owners."

"I see; I think I'm beginning to understand," she said. What she was beginning to understand was that like most irreconcilable social debates, the opposing sides each based their arguments on totally incompatible values. There could never be a meeting of minds through reason because the belief systems were too different. Those opposed to cockfights believed the human soul was degraded by blood sport and that chickens could feel pain. Those in favor of cockfights believed the birds' nobility inspired human nobility and if chickens bled they did not suffer. Those opposed had their laws; those in favor didn't enforce those laws. Society once again was muddling through an irreconcilable difference simply by ignoring the whole thing, for the most part. Society usually worked best when it worked sloppily. Yes, she was starting to understand, if not approve. What she didn't understand, however, is why any owner would agree to a mismatch. Why did Powers pit a small bird against that Polish?

"Here, Molly, you want a smoke?" Paul said.

"Thank you, no."

Just then there was a roar from inside.

"Somethin's happened."

"I'd better get back to Louella," said Molly.

Louella stood by the pit, grinning. "The Polish is winning," she said. "I thought it had a weight advantage; weight'll beat ever' time, but that Powers bird's fighting style had me concerned thar fer a minute."

The Powers bird lay, mangled as a roadkill, on the ground. The Polish, bloody and tired, was still standing. The referee picked it up, held it over his head and announced it was the winner. Scowling people began handing money to grinners. Louella grinned even wider as J.B. handed her $40. By the time everyone had paid her, she held $200.

"I bet four to one," she laughed.

"Meaning you bet the whole fifty on this first match."

"Course."

"Listen, I've heard a few things," Molly said. "I think we should get while the getting is good."

"Just one more."

"Louella, I don't like this place."

The old woman was torn. "Have you found out why Butcher Cook is here?" Louella said.

"Butcher? Here? No."

"Yes, that real strange. I just saw Dow hand the dead bird to him. Supper, I reckon. But why's he here?"

"Where is he?"

"Over thar at Powers' table."

New birds had been set on the inspection tables. And betting this time was, judging by the banter, going heavily against the Powers bird. "I wonder if that first fight was a ringer," Louella said.

"What?"

"Set to make it look like Powers' birds hada lost it. Sometimes a real good line get so good no one will bet against, so have to run a rigged fight to git interest sparky agin."

"Now what's Butcher doing?" Molly said.

He was making his way across the shed to the challenger's table. He left behind him those tracks again. She looked at the feet of others in the crowd. Nikes. Reeboks. Some boots. Every shoe or boot left treadmarks. Herringbones. Dots. Wedges. Stripes. Squiggles. Only Butcher's shoeprints were smooth. When he reached the table, Butcher petted the bird.

"We need to inspect that bird," Louella said.

Louella said hello to Butcher, who didn't seem to remember

her, but being Butcher, he greeted every stranger with a big smile.

"What's this bird?" Louella asked him.

"My pretty bird. He mine."

"Really?"

"He all mine."

"May I hold him?" Louella said.

She cooed and praised the bird and told Butcher what a pretty rooster he had. The handler stood by wordlessly, grinning, but saying nothing. When they stepped away from the table, Louella said, "I think that's City Chicken."

"How do you know?"

"It's missing a toe and folks say City Chicken had lost a toe somewhar."

"But why would anybody want an untrained bird in these fights? It'd be at a disadvantage."

"Mebbe that's why. It's heavier than the Powers bird, but without experience it'll be at a disadvantage against a canny rooster. Kids'll go without groceries this month; this fight is rigged."

"Is it Powers that's rigging it?"

"Molly, hush, someone'll hear. Yore right; let's git."

They headed for the door.

"Leavin' already, Louella?" the old doorkeeper called.

"Not as young as I used to be, but I be back next week. If'n I can get this city gal t'bring me."

"Next one's next Sunday morning, okay? And where's told the usual way."

"Right; I know. See you."

22

SUCH A NIGHT

The moon, surprisingly bright for half full, easily lit their way back to Matins' hidden truck. A few clouds, the remnants of the day's rain, shuttered a few stars, but otherwise the sky was clear and the ground dry. Weedy, but dry. Matins slowly pulled out of his hiding spot. The truck jounced lightless for a stretch, then he turned them on.

"Driving wi'out lights is one o' them country boy skills," Louella said to Molly. "You learn it from running moonshine."

Matins laughed.

"You ever do that, John?" Molly said.

Matins laughed again but didn't answer. He did tell them he had called the state police and asked them to watch the two ends of Slim's road for him, but not to do anything unless he told them to. He also said he'd called his two deputies first to be sure they were on duty.

"I told them once if they ever missed a Saturday night again, first I'd kill 'em, then I'd fire 'em. Molly, I like this phone; they thought with both cruisers there, I couldn't hassle them." Matins turned onto the main road and spotted one of the highway patrol cars. He stopped and chatted awhile.

"Why don't they raid the game?" Molly wanted to know, when he climbed back in the truck.

They had better things to do, he explained, bigger crimes to chase than some good ol' boy thing. As long as the pit didn't get too rowdy, most police, state or local, in most counties, left them alone. Him included.

"More important crimes like what?" Molly said.

"We keep pretty busy Saturday nights," he said. "Barfights mostly; Saturday night is fight night or beat the wife and kids night. After the bars is when most women get their bruises for the week." He looked grim. "And there's a few other minor things."

"Like loose dogs?" Molly teased.

He smiled, but it was a sad smile, "Like convenience-store holdups, vandalizing cemeteries and such, car stealing, and, sure, loose dogs. Loose dogs kill sheep, you know."

"What d'we do now?" Louella wanted to know.

"Well, for one thing you can give me back my fifty dollars," Matins said. With a flourish, she handed him sixty.

"What's this?"

"Your share o' the winnings."

"My *share?*"

"And, Molly, here's fifty fer you. Rest is mine."

"The *rest?*"

"She's keeping ninety for herself," Molly said.

"Wish I'd know'd you back when," Matins said, shaking his head.

The three compared theories as they drove, Molly still calling their candidates "suspects," Louella calling them "orn'ry sorts," while to Matins they were just "boys to talk to." As the only professional present, he had to be, well, professional. But whatever the term, they all agreed Dave Breyers and Bill

Winthrop were not suspects, orn'ry or in line for a talking to anymore, but that J.B. III, Wrongbutton, Butcher Cook and now Tom Powers were suspiciously orn'ry and ought to be tops on a list for conversations.

"A list?" Molly said, brightening. She pulled out her Saturday list from her purse, ready to add to it.

"I should've known never to use that word 'round a list-maker." Matins groaned.

"You a listmaker?" Louella said. Molly nodded, waving it. "Me too. Every day or once a week?"

"Every day," Molly said.

"I do mine oncet a week," said Louella. "Do you group items or jist list 'em?"

"Just list."

"I'm the category type. Do you number things or dot 'em?"

"Ladies, please," Matins protested.

"Dot them," Molly said.

"And don't call us ladies," Louella added.

"Female temporary colleagues, then; let's get to work here."

"Okay, what's first?" Molly said.

"Well first," Matins said sheepishly, "what's the *Far Side* cartoon for today?"

"See?" Molly said to Louella, "He growls a lot but underneath he's almost human." Molly described it. A deer was cringing behind a tree, hiding from a hunter and thinking, No doubt about it, he is trying to kill me. Do I know this guy? I've got to *think*.

"How'd you do today?" Louella said.

"Well,•Help Dave with his computer. Did that.•Funeral. Did that. But the rest is not done.•Help with Meal Van booth. •Bathe dogs.•Haircut if time.•Clean—"

"You *still* don't have that haircut?" Matins said.

"No time," Molly said.

"We bin keepin' her busy chasin' murderers," Louella said.

"Okay, we've got to *think*," Matins said. "What do we know so far?"

"About Butcher?" Molly said.

"Yeah, let's start there," Matins said. "We know he's probably the chicken thief and that it's Powers who's taught him to steal."

"But why? Powers must have hundreds of his own chickens," Molly said.

"Powers needed opponents for them rigged matches, ordinary barnyard roosters, not bred fighters," Louella said.

"Still," Matins countered, "he must have less aggressive roosters among his breeding stock. If he needs them, why steal them? Put a dot by that, Molly."

"Anything else on Butcher?" she said.

"I can't imagine how Powers persuaded him," Matins said.

"I can," Molly said. "Butcher's learned that roadkill is okay; I remember thinking how much like roadkill the losing chicken looked; all Powers had to do was tell him these were roadkills."

"No, I meant persuaded him to steal."

"That's how; first, Butcher loves attention; second, he trusted Powers after Powers gave him roadkill, so I'm sure Butcher did anything he asked after that."

"He seem real attached to that City Chicken, though, almost his pet," Louella said. "Wonder how he's going to feel when it gits hurt or killed tonight."

"Maybe we should have stayed a little longer?" Molly said.

No one commented on that.

"So what do we know about Wrongbutton?" Molly said, making a new box on her list. "That he announces the fights, and that he might have been having an affair with Cathy. Anything else?"

"No, except if Cathy was about to dump him, as she was inclined to do, he'd have motive," Matins said.

"Thought you didn't believe in motive," Molly said.

"They's only two motives," Louella said, "love and money. Wrongbutton's love."

"And Powers is money for sure," Molly said. "My gossiping smoking club—"

"Smoking club?"

"The guys outside I overheard. They said that fighting line was being bred by both of them. So it must have been Powers who was paying that ten percent."

"And who was so far behind in his payments Cathy had to be angry with him," Matins said. If he hadn't been driving, he would have been pulling on his lip, Molly thought.

"I think I know now what those strange boxes were in the *Chicks* file—records of crosses, which cock to which hen and how the offspring performed," she said.

"So if'n its Wrongbutton for love and Powers for money, which one done it?" Louella said.

"There's still that mysterious 'lover before Wrongbutton' too," Matins said.

"J.B.?"

"Mebbe. He was thar at the funeral; he do play around too. Mebbe she disappoint him and he got violent," Louella said.

"But I've never known him to hurt a woman," Matins said. "He's a real dedicated sexist. Only beats up men."

"Mebbe they all done it," Louella said.

Others not totally off their list, they agreed, were any of the pit hosts, such as Jacob Cory, Slim Coolis, Bennett Williams. Also, anyone who'd lost big or lost consistently was a possibility, they agreed. But Molly couldn't remember any names on the printouts that showed frequent losses, still assuming those lists were losses, not winnings.

"So back to my house to look at lists?" Louella said.

"No, I'm worried about Wrongbutton," Matins said. "If Molly's gossip group is right, he's in big trouble. Nothing's going to happen to him while he's at the pit, but after's another thing."

"Where's he going to go when he leaves?" Molly asked.

"If he's winning, to a bar; he loses, home."

"He's losing, then," said Louella. "He's in Powers' trap. He bet heavily on the Powers bird first match. When we left I heerd him dickering with someone on that ringer, that City Chicken."

"Molly, punch the Redial button on that phone," Matins said. "Should go right to state police headquarters, let me talk to them."

He told the dispatcher to get Porter Wilton-Jones' license number and tell the spotter cars to watch for his truck.

"No, don't arrest him, just watch where he goes . . . Well, yes, you idjit, then call me and tell me which way he went. What'd you think I wanted to know fer? . . . Yeah, so's you'rn."

"You'rn what?" Louella wanted to know, as he handed the phone back to Molly.

"Now, Louella, contrary to some people's notions, I still say you're a lady."

"I'm not," Molly said. "You'rn what?"

Matins had turned for Angel Ridge. Wrongbutton's trailer was a country stone's throw from the station, a country stone's throw being like a country mile, lots longer than a regular one, but not all that far. Matins decided to park behind the transmitter to be close, but out of sight. "I should take you two home, but I'm afraid if I do, I'll miss him. Damn, I should have put you in the patrol car when I was there. Didn't think of it."

"We wouldn'ta gone."

"Louella, I *am* the sheriff. I can make you do things if'n I want."

"Johnny, man ain't been born who kin—"

The phone beeped. Molly jumped half a foot. She'd never heard it before because no one had ever called her on it before, not even Ken.

"I think it's for you," she said, handling it over to Matins.

"Hi . . . Yeah . . . No, but I may need you yet, don't go out for no jelly doughnuts . . . Wrongbutton's driving this way, they say," he said as Molly replaced the phone in her purse.

"How'd you get my phone number?"

"Easy, there's a button displays your number when you punch it."

"For heaven's sake, I never knew that," Molly said.

"Okay, you two. Out of the truck," Matins said.

"No," Louella said.

"Yes. I want to talk to him alone and without civilians. Having you along could not only get me a reprimand, but if Wrongbutton's not pure as a lily, and good chance he ain't, your being present could be legal trouble later, jeopardize the People's case, you know. That's you. You'ns are the people, I reckon."

Molly helped a sulky Louella out. "Wait here, I'll get you in about a half-hour."

The two sat on the steps to the studio. "Think it's true whut he say 'bout us a jeopardy and all?" Louella said.

"Probably not," Molly said, "but he's a native, so he can tell a good lie when he has to."

"I say we should walk over there," Louella said.

"I say we should be sensible and wait right here," Molly said.

Another pickup drove by just then, going fast.

"Louella, how's your eyesight?"

"Good."

"Who do you think was in that truck? J.B.?"

"Nope."

"Powers?"

"Yep."

"Did he have anyone with him?

"Yep."

"J.B.?"

"Nope."

"Who, then?"

"Butcher."

"Butcher?"

"Yep, but I'm not a' worried 'bout Butcher near so much I am 'bout that gun he ha' on his gunrack."

"I didn't see any gun."

"I did."

23

Directions

The two women sat in troubled silence a moment, both staring with no particular focus at the weed-flecked parking lot in front of the studio. The steps they sat on were store bought and eight inches too short for the job of reaching the trailer's door. Beyond the gravel, vigorous, knee-high weeds claimed the neutral space left by road, ditch or woods around the trailer.

"We're not even sure he's going to Wrongbutton's," Molly said. "Could have just been passing by."

"If'n it's money, he has motive," Louella said.

"Maybe he's just going to tell Wrongbutton where the next fight is."

"If'n it's love mebbe he has motive too. Mebbe he's that mysterious lover before Wrongbutton ever'body so worried about. And he do be carrying a shotgun in that truck."

"Lots of people carry guns," Molly said.

"Not many do this time o' year. For love or money, I think we should go help Johnny," Louella said.

"John'll be madder than a springtailed hornet if we go up there and there's no need."

"Springtailed hornet?" Louella said.

"Hopping mad."

Silence again. Then Louella said, "Maybe he's not in trouble, but ain't you just dyin' to know whut's going on?"

"Can you walk that far?"

Louella puckered her lips. "No harm trying." The two plunged into the weeds in I'm-not-afraid-of-snakes style, Louella stumping along heavily but surprisingly quickly on her cane. Soon, however, she was breathing hard. "You go ahaid; I catch up."

Three pickups, Wrongbutton's, Matins' and Powers', clustered around the door of the rusting and dented trailer that was Wrongbutton's home. Butcher was leaning on Powers' truck. When Molly stepped from the weeds, he brightened as usual to see a face he knew and started to yell out a greeting.

"Shh," Molly said.

"Shh, shh, be quiet," Butcher replied. Loudly. Molly groaned. So much for surprise.

"Go help Louella," she said. "She's back there. She needs you."

Fortunately, no one inside had heard Butcher because both Powers and Wrongbutton were shouting. Molly stood to one side and peeked through the trailer screen. She could see Powers pointing a shotgun at Wrongbutton, who stood at the far side of the room. Matins was on the couch but his pistol was tossed on the floor at Powers' feet. Despite being disarmed, Matins sat almost calmly on the edge of the sofa, pulling thoughtfully on his lip. Wrongbutton was shrieking.

"I never carried on with her; we went for beers a few times, but why not, we was working together."

"She give you money?" Powers said.

"Of course, seein' as I was announcing your fights, you know. She paid me for that; only fair don't you think? I certainly didn't kill her. And I warn't her lover, though wouldn'ta minded if I'da bin. She war right pretty."

"You kill her, Tom?" Matins said quietly to Powers.

"She war steppin' out on me," Powers said. "She war all dressed up for Wrongbutton to come. Not for me. But I didn't kill her; he did. And I'm going to kill him, going to do tonight what I shoulda done that night his pa was shot. My brother went to jail for shooting the wrong bastard."

"You and Cathy weren't getting along, were you?" Matins said to Powers. Molly wondered how he could be so calm with a shotgun waving in front of him.

"Bitch was skewing all the records."

"How?"

"She kept the records on her damn computer, which bird won, lost, and why. We'd bred 'em specialized for fighting style, but I couldn't tell which bird was which without those records. She gave me bogus data one night. I lost near every fight."

"Which is why you needed Butcher to steal some roosters for you," Matins said. "You didn't know tonight which birds of yours were the good ones."

"Wrongbutton told you a lot before I got here, didn't he?"

"Nope, figured most of this on my own. What was Cathy's role in all this, besides records, I mean?"

"She suggested most of the crosses. She bought chicks from all over the country for the mixes. My line was really hers; I provided the land and the front. No man'd let a woman set up fights, especially down in Kentucky or West Virginia."

"Well, Tom, I agree with you. I don't think you killed her; I think Wrongbutton did," Matins said.

"I didn't."

"But you were there that night, weren't you?" Matins said to Wrongbutton.

"Yes, 'bout seven-thirty as usual. She was dead then and I ran, scared. But I didn't kill her."

"Computer says she was alive at seven-ten."

"I don't know much about computers," Wrongbutton said,

"but that seven-ten means somebody fiddled with it, not Cathy, mebbe the killer. I do know she was dead at seven-thirty and I didn't kill her."

"Hush you. Give me your gun, Tom. Let me take care of Wrongbutton. I take care of it, it'll end here. You take care of it and you know the Wilton-Jones clan'll wipe out your whole family. You kill Wrongbutton, you just be signing a death warrant for you and your brothers too."

"No, Matins, you're a good man and I hate to hurt you, but the law just dallies and locks 'em up a little and coddles 'em. You two have to disappear."

Molly pulled the phone from her purse and hit the Redial button, tiptoeing away from the door to be out of hearing. "On Angel Ridge, about a quarter mile past the transmitter. And hurry. Two men are held hostage at gunpoint. . . . No, no, on the left . . . No, on the left if you're going *away* from town. . . . No, away from town *toward* Kentucky. No, *past* Dutch Ridge . . . No, no, landmarks; it's just woods. If you see farms, you're on the wrong road . . . No . . . No . . . Dammit, get a map. Two men are in serious danger here. Hurry."

Just then Louella and Butcher crashed through the weeds. This time Powers did hear the noise and turned for the door. Matins lunged for his pistol and missed. Powers reacted by flipping his shotgun around, clubbing Matins with the stock, and knocking him unconscious.

"Butcher, what are you doing?" Powers yelled through the screen.

"Helpin' Miz Louella."

Powers slammed open the screen. "What in hell's tarnation is *she* doing here?"

Louella, for once, didn't have a good lie handy, but stood leaning on her cane, breathing heavily.

Powers was beginning to panic. The quiet murder he'd planned was getting too crowded. Still cradling the shotgun, he got some nylon baling twine from his truckbed and tied up first

Wrongbutton and then Louella. He made Wrongbutton climb in the truck and then tied his feet. Then he lifted Louella in. Next he went inside and tied up Matins. Butcher wanted to know why Matins was sleeping.

He told Butcher to help him carry Matins, but John was too heavy for them. His breath rasping from panic, Powers abandoned that idea and left Matins unconscious on Wrongbutton's floor.

"Okay, Butcher, you climb in the truckbed," Powers said.

"Is Miz Molly coming too?" Butcher said cheerfully.

Powers' eyes opened wide. "Molly? She here too?" he roared. "Where is she?"

Powers stood a second, trying to get control of his breathing, then told Butcher to guard Louella and Wrongbutton while he looked for Molly. She heard all this from the weeds where she had hidden. He's trying to shoot me all right, she thought. I've got to *think*. As quietly as she could, she pushed deeper into the brush, wondering which was worse, Powers with a shotgun, or the certain poison ivy and snakes in the woods.

Powers headed into the same woods. She circled stealthily in the opposite direction, thinking, I am less afraid of snakes than I am of crazed chicken breeders.

"Butcher," she could hear Louella shrieking, "you untie me right this minute, y'hear?"

"Mr. Powers he said not to."

"Why you mind him? He a bad man."

Molly slipped up to the truck. "Hush," she said, slipping into the driver's seat. "If he stops looking for me we're in even bigger trouble."

Butcher had begun to tremble.

"Have I been bad?" he cried.

24

HOTWIRE

Damn, no keys," Molly said. Now she was beginning to panic too.

"He took all three sets; he's got all the keys," Wrongbutton said.

"Wrongbutton, you know how to hotwire, don't you?" Louella said.

"Sure do," he said, holding his hands out for Molly to untie. Her reasoning was split-second but complicated: Matins thinks Wrongbutton is the killer. It's safer to have a killer tied up. Which is worse, a killer with a shotgun or a killer untied who's willing to hotwire you out of here? Easy choice. She pulled at the twine.

Wrongbutton bent under the dash, bumping his head sharply as he did so. He pulled out the ignition wires and crossed them expertly. "These older trucks are so much easier; wires right handy," he commented as the engine fired. Molly hoped Powers didn't hear the roar.

"Another one of those country-boy skills," Louella said as Molly pulled out of the yard. "Attagal, no lights," she added.

"Yeah, any country boy knows hotwiring." Wrongbutton beamed with professional pride.

"What about John?" Louella said.

"One rescue at a time," Molly rasped. Driving without lights, she'd just discovered, took concentration. She checked the rearview mirror to see if Powers were following and saw instead that Butcher had jumped in the truckbed and was delightedly watching the passing scenery. Such an innocent, she thought. He has no idea what's happening.

"He was going to shoot me and then have Butcher handle the gun," Wrongbutton said as he untied Louella's arms and rubbed them for her to restore circulation. He was shaking as if realization were just sinking in. "He wanted to get Butcher's fingerprints on it so he'd be blamed for both murders. If Matins hadn't been there I'd be dead now."

"Weird plot," Molly said. "Butcher doesn't drive. Wouldn't people know he couldn't get to the Mill or your trailer without help?"

"Now, Molly," Louella said. "If the man is too stupid to hatch his own chickens, he's too stupid to hatch a good murder plot."

She'd reached the studio. "Wrongbutton, call and keep calling the state police until those clowns get here."

"Clowns?" Louella said.

"I've been taking Appalachian vocabulary lessons," Molly said.

"From Johnny?"

"No, from the McKennas." Wrongbutton had lifted Louella to the ground and helped Butcher from the truckbed. Butcher must have picked up Louella's cane because he now handed it to her with a big smile. Molly put the truck into reverse. "Now, all of you, stay hid," she yelled, and started to drive away.

"Where you going?" Louella cried.

"Back for John."

"Molly, you're crazy," Wrongbutton bellowed.

She thought about that for half a second. "Yes. I am," she said slowly. Almost like a native. Then, tires spitting gravel, she spun the truck around and leapt out of the lot. She did that almost like a native too.

Powers was still thrashing through the woods looking for her. The racket he made covered the hum of the truck. Inside, John was groggily coming to on the floor. She began to untie him. But now the truck's engine started to idle roughly, almost to a stall. If she didn't get John into it now, they'd be stuck here. Well, maybe John knew hotwiring too.

"Please wake up, John." She shook him, then tried to help him sit up. He sat a moment but was too dizzy to stay up. He flopped to his side, then tried again to lift up, but flopped again, groaning. Molly tried to hold him up, but he was too big for her to manage. A concussion? Or worse? she worried. She went to the kitchen to get some ice for him. Where are those damn state police? she fumed. Lost, no doubt. Everyone gets lost on these roads. "Please come to, John," she said. "We've got to get out of here now."

She heard the truck cough and stop. The thrashing in the woods had stopped too. The silence made her skin crawl. Even the katydids seemed still.

With a bang, loud as a shot, the screen door slammed open. Powers.

"Oh. Hi," Molly said. "Did your bird win the second fight?"

25

SMALL TALK

Where's Wrongbutton?" Powers snarled, waving his shotgun at them.

"Escaped," Molly said.

"Louella?"

"More of the same."

"Butcher?"

Molly shrugged. "John and I are here," she said sweetly. Whether Matins was appalled by her banter or too groggy to react, she couldn't say, but he stayed quiet. If only I can keep Powers talking until the police arrive, she thought. But how do you make small talk with a psychotic?

"So, your family been in this area long?" she said.

"Un-hm," Powers said.

Ouch, makes Charlotte seem voluble, Molly thought.

"So, what do you raise on your farm, besides chickens, I mean."

He frowned quizzically at her, wondering no doubt why she wanted to chat. John frowned too, either from the pain of the head blow or in disapproval of her tactics. Maybe both. "Beagles, a few horses," Powers said cautiously. Molly wondered if she'd skidded over the line of Appalachian etiquette. As manners go here, it was okay to point a shotgun at someone, but ask a direct question, no.

"Sounds like a lovely place, how much acreage do you have?" There, that was a bit more discreet. Maybe he would go for that.

" 'Bout a hundred fifty acres are mine."

"Your brothers farm too?"

"Un-hm."

What was the right question with this man? Try family again. "Your folks come here during the mining boom?"

"Nope. 'Fore that. 'Fore the Civil War."

"Really? From abroad or from the States?"

"From Virginia. We're part Virginia aristocrat, part Cherokee. That's why we had to come out here. Family didn't approve of that Cherokee. Out here, folks didn't care. Mixed bloods were welcome. There are whole towns near our farm, ghost towns now, called WIN towns, for white, Indian, Negro, where folks got along no matter what color; they married, they lived together. This is a good place for mixed bloods. My great-great-great-grandmother was a fullblooded Cherokee and she brung in a lot of the Indians that are still here."

"Cherokee, not Shawnee?" said Molly, relieved to finally have him talking. Yes, ancestor questions were almost always the right thing to do. "Cherokee?" she repeated.

"Yeah, Shawnee gone, all gone from here by the 1830s. This be in the 1850s or so when she came. She's buried on the place, we got our own cemetery up there, all my folks buried there. I wanted to be buried there too. I wanted to rest there someday."

"Wanted? You sound like you think you won't."

He sat down, a troubled man, his face furrowed with pain, but he still pointed the gun at them. "I got a note due, overdue actually. Six generations on that land we've been, and I'm the one that's agoin' to lose it."

"I thought your farm was doing okay."

"No. I'm deep in debt. Chicken prices have fallen. Feed prices risen. Without those pits I'd have lost it a year ago."

"That's why you were behind on payments to Cathy, you were paying off your notes." So Louella was wrong; it wasn't love or money, it was land, Molly thought. "You were going to lose your land if your cockpit operation failed?"

"And the cemetery and all my—my history. So peaceful there. There's dogwoods she planted, my Cherokee grandma. She'd go hunting in the woods, not for meat, but for tree saplings. I like to think of her doing that, like to imagine her still walking these woods looking fer things, herbs and such. I go to her grave a lot so I can talk wi' her. All the graves there lay east–west on top our highest hill. See, folks here b'lieve the Second Coming's going to come from the east and the dead'll see it first if they's buried facing east. I . . . she . . . had the means to destroy all that."

"She being Cathy?" Molly said. Matins was now listening intently, but carefully not moving. Anything to keep him talking.

"I didn't mind her steppin' out on me—well, I minded it, but I figured that's women. And I figured she had a right to nag about the money seein' as how I did owe it to her, but when she put the kibosh on those matches and make it so it could lose me my land, I got so angry, I don't even remember putting the gun in my hand. I just, 'fore I knowed it I was standing there with a hot shotgun and she was blown dead. I ran. I passed Wrong-button going out. I thought he seen me."

"You know you can't kill anymore, Tom," Molly said softly. "It's no solution; it makes it worse. You kill a lawman and the whole United States would go looking for you."

His face was flushed, red again with panic.

"Why don't you just go, get away before the police get here," she continued, still softly.

"If'n I flee I may get away but that's as good as never seeing my land again."

"If you don't go, it's the same, Tom. Just put the gun down and go."

"What'll happen to my wife, my family?"

"Folks'll help them. Go. Police are on the way. Better go while you can."

John was tensely conscious now. Molly saw his eyes stray to his gun still lying on the floor. Oh no, I'm an idiot, Molly thought. Why didn't I think to pick it up? First thing a pro would have done is get that gun. Me, no, I've got to play little nursie and get a stupid ice cup.

Powers too had followed Matins' glance and now saw the handgun again. He picked it up and made a decision. "Both of you into the truck," he said. Molly winced. She was sure she'd almost persuaded him to flee.

She helped John stand. He was dizzy, but otherwise seemed okay. He said nothing but leaned on Molly's shoulder as they moved toward the door. Molly stepped out first, followed by John, then Powers. As Powers's foot hit the step, a cane flashed, hooking his legs, then flashed again, hooking his shotgun. As he fell, the handgun flew away into the weeds.

Molly turned. All she had seen was the cane. She knew it was Louella's and figured Wrongbutton had borrowed it. But no, it was Louella, who now was holding the shotgun and from the firm look on her face was intending to use it. And well knew how, too.

"Louella, don't shoot that gun. It should be fired by a laboratory if it's the murder weapon," Matins gasped, and then he fainted.

Such a professional, Molly thought.

"How'd you get back here?" she said to Louella.

"Walked."

"Where's Wrongbutton?"

"At the studio. He pulled an amp or somesich thing on his haid and conked hisself out. I left Butcher awatching him."

Molly found some cuffs in Matins' pickup. Tears streamed

down Powers' face as she cuffed him to the truckbed, but otherwise he was quiet. In the distance they heard sirens. "I think from the sound, they're on Dutchman's Ridge," Molly said.

"I know'd they'd git lost," Louella said. "Ever'body does."

"Is there really a Dutchman the ridge was named for?" Molly asked.

"No, they's Germans."

"Ah, so Dutch is a corruption of Deutsch," Molly said.

"Whatever," Louella said. She handed the shotgun to Molly, used her cane to lower herself down by Matins and ran her hands expertly over his skull with the same thoroughness with which she'd handled the chickens. "He probably does have a concussion," she said. "Best for that is to stay real quiet, git home and git in bed and stay thar. Too much stirrin' around maybe cause swellin' and that kin be serious."

A state patrol car pulled up. Matins was shakily coming to and coherent enough to negotiate the arrest with the two officers, who took Powers away.

Wrongbutton and Butcher then walked up. Wrongbutton sported a couple of goose eggs on his forehead. After getting the facts he'd need for Monday morning's newscast, he offered to take Butcher home.

Molly, Matins and Louella got into Matins' pickup; Molly drove. First stop, Louella's.

"What's going to happen to Butcher?" Molly asked. "I really think everything he did was because Powers told him to. He isn't capable of imagining stealing."

"Well, he won't be prosecuted probably, because he's not competent to stand trial," Matins said. He was leaning against the back window of the cab and looked as if he had a colossal headache, which he probably did. "But he's a ward of the state. They'll probably want to take him out of the halfway house and put him in something more secure, so he can't come and go as he pleases so much."

"He'd die," Molly said. "He's such a free spirit."

Louella said, "I kin take care of it."

"How?" Matins asked.

"I'll jist call ever'one who's lost a chicken and convince 'em they hain't lost a chicken. You two ain't heerd of no chickens bein' stolen, have you?"

"Course not." Matins smiled, then winced.

"Everyone'll agree to that?" Molly said.

"Course they will. Butcher was used; he shouldn't be shut up jist b'cause someone else tore on his innocence. I'll make those calls in the morning."

26

RIBBONS

Molly called Ken from the truck as she drove.

"Do you know the time?" he said.

"No, what is it?"

"It's after one-thirty. Where were you? I've been worried to death. I called Louella's and no answer. I called your cellular phone and got John. He said you were out and could he take a message? I said, not funny. Then he said not to call again, the phone was for official police business only."

Molly laughed. "On top of that he forgot to give me your message. I've been to a cockfight. I won, too," she bragged, and then asked him to meet her at the Matins' because John was hurt and would need some help getting from the truck to the house.

"I don't need no help," John growled as she shut off the phone.

"Don't be stubborn, or I'll—"

"Or you'll what?"

"Or I'll call you Johnny."

Betty was anxiously waiting in their drive, Ken behind her, as Molly pulled in. Goldie and the puppy were there too. Goldie tried to waggle a greeting when she saw Molly, but was hampered by the puppy chewing on her ear. The three of them helped John to a couch.

Betty first called the doctor. "John, he wants to know was there any bleeding from your ears, nose or mouth? No? Good . . . Molly, check his pupils, he says; are they unequal in size?"

Molly looked; John stuck out his tongue. To Betty she shook her head no.

"Pupils okay," Betty said into the phone, "Dizziness? At first; seems gone now, right, John? . . . Nausea? . . . No? He says no; can we count my stomachache from worrying about him as nausea? . . . No, just pain in the butt? Doctor, where did you study anatomy? . . . Headache?" John held his hands out about a yard apart. "Yes, a big one he says . . . Facial muscle spasms?" John lolled his tongue and twitched his cheeks. "No, he's normal as a petunia. 'Bout as sweet as one too."

As she hung up, Betty reported, "He says since he lost consciousness twice that's bad, but since there's no bleeding or nausea or pupil irregularity that's good, so he's probably got a mild concussion and the best thing is to stay put. Sitting in the car to get to a hospital be worse than staying put right now. He says you're to lie down and stay down, y'hear me?"

"Yes'm," he said. "I'll be good. Don't feel much like dancing anyways."

"Doctor said keep him quiet, give him all the ice he wants. If he keeps complaining of dizziness or starts throwing up, to first call an ambulance, then him. Thank God it's something minor, this time."

Minor? Molly thought. Watching them, she wondered how often there were nights like this, the worry, the conference with the doctor, the relief. He had a dangerous job. Every Saturday night must be hell for her.

Betty plied everyone with ice, in a bag for John's head, in soft drinks for the rest of them. Then Molly, helped here and there with embellishments from John, told the whole adventure, from printouts to cane. John's comment at the end was he thought Molly would make a pretty good deputy, *if* she took a police science course or two over at Hocking Tech in Athens County where first thing they teach you is "Pick up the gun, stupid."

As the story wound down, Betty darted into the kitchen and returned carrying a red ribbon.

"This is yours," she said to Molly.

"What?"

"Your beans won a ribbon today."

"You picked and entered my beans?"

"Yes." Betty was glowing with pride for her star gardening pupil.

"I know blue means first, but what does red mean?" Molly said.

"Second."

"I won second?" She smiled, then frowned. "Wait, how many entries? Two?"

"No, twelve. Beans were real popular, so second is really good."

"Well, how about that?" Molly said, shyly pleased. "And who won first?"

Betty hung her head. "I did," she said. "But wait, I did it fair. I picked your beans first and I picked the best. Then I picked mine. I just beat you is all."

Molly laughed.

"Done enough tramping through weeds tonight," Molly grumbled to Ken as they walked the path back to their own house. Ken held her tightly about the waist with one arm and swung a flashlight with the other. Molly was carrying the exhausted and soundly sleeping puppy. Goldie ranged ahead. "I'm as tired as this puppy. What a day," she said.

Ken had been silent during most of the storytelling, but now he had comments and questions galore and little of it was about the murder. "I had no idea you were in danger until it was all over," he said, "and yet I'm all shaky inside just thinking about it. You could have been killed. How does Betty live with that fear week after week?"

"I'm seeing them both in whole new ways after today," Molly said.

"Promise me never to take a risk like that again; I can't lose you."

"I didn't plan to get in trouble tonight. Things just happened," she said.

"I'll admit to mixed feelings here," Ken said. "I don't know whether I'm relieved you're safe, angry you got in danger, or envious that you were at a real cockfight. What did you think of it?"

"The bloodiness bothered me a lot; my stomach was heaving the whole time," Molly said. "But if you ignore that part of it, it was just one big party, and the people were just people. Nothing sinister about them. They were just having fun. Most were friendly to me. If they could find another kind of entertainment, I'd go to another party with them. Why can't they do country line dancing instead?"

"A good question. So many paradoxes here. Molly, do you know what's happened to you tonight? I saw it when John just now helped embellish your story. You were just like Geertz telling his story. People won't be 'away' around you anymore. By the time Louella and Wrongbutton get through telling about tonight, everybody will be wanting you to tell about it. You'll belong here after tonight. Wonder how it will change things for you? Wish I could have seen what you've seen tonight."

"And taken notes?"

He laughed softly. "You still mad about that?"

"No, I think I understand it better now. I mean, Louella did give me a choice there to go in or not and I did say yes. I felt what you must feel. I wanted to know. I wanted to see. But I can't say I understood what I saw."

"Too many paradoxes?"

"Yes, good people, bad fun. It was so easy yesterday to be horrified and condemn cockfighting. I'm still horrified, but now I see their need to be inspired, to have some reason to get up in the morning against all odds. I can't condemn that need."

"The curse of insight," Ken said. "Makes us tolerate too much, doesn't it?"

"Maybe. I wish they had another source of inspiration."

"Did you see those clan tensions I told you about?" Ken asked.

"I don't know. I really wasn't sure who was related to whom. Wrongbutton seemed to hold away from the others, but I thought that was grief for Cathy."

"If Cathy had put the energy she spent on that cockfighting ring into a legitimate business, she'd be alive today, maybe rich, too," Ken said.

"She may be the biggest paradox in this," Molly said.

"I don't think so," Ken said. "Maybe she was a typical Appalachian woman taught from girlhood not to be independent. Look at how local women fear your independence; look how long it took Betty to decide she could manage that job. Cathy was just the same, afraid to be successful because women aren't supposed to be. No, you want paradox, I nominate Powers."

"I actually felt sorry for him when I clipped him to the truck," Molly said. "I mean, he'd killed someone and might have killed me or the others, but yet I understood him, I understood what drove him. Loss. Fear of loss."

"Of losing the land?"

"Yes, but didn't he know bankers are willing to negotiate? Why didn't he talk with his bankers instead?"

"Maybe his notes weren't with banks," Ken said.

"Oh, I didn't think of that."

"Odd how both he and Wrongbutton have an ancestor who is almost real to them, who still lives in their imaginations," Ken said.

"Powers said he talks to his Cherokee grandmother."

"Maybe that's why clan ties are so strong here. The personalities of the ancestors are remembered, not just their names. Makes it hard to leave them or betray them."

"Maybe Powers is not such a paradox, after all," Molly said.

"We're so clever; we've eliminated all paradoxes," Ken said.

"Except Louella. I needed a scorecard for her," Molly said. "My pictures of her are all at odds—the responsible, competent county commissioner; the proper housewife who crochets and raises children and dotes on her husband; this bloodthirsty gambler; and a tigress with a cane in a crisis. Which is the real Louella?"

"Perhaps all of them," Ken said. "Appalachian women survive by a surface docility and an underlying toughness. You saw the toughness at the pit and on Angel Ridge tonight. The gambler might have been just a lonely woman longing for her husband or revisiting her past. Either way, she's a classic example of Appalachian dualism."

"But why does dual passivity and strength produce in Louella an interesting and effective woman but a doomed and destructive one in Cathy?"

"There's the essential paradox," Ken said. "Culture shapes individuals, but it doesn't determine character. Good and evil are produced by all cultures."

"Loss, then, if Powers is typical, must be culture's driving force," Molly said.

Ken thought about that for a moment. "Wow, I like that, sounds like a title for a paper. 'Loss, colon, the Barometer of Appalachian Experience.' It has to have a colon or it's not an academic paper."

"Yes, I know, I know. One more paradox to figure in all this," Molly said, "is what Louella's doing for Butcher. Remember how you said there are no communities here?"

"Yes."

"But she's going to call all those people who've lost chickens. She's doing it to help someone who's not a relative, not a friend, not even a neighbor. If that's not community, what is?"

"Well, as I also said, more research is needed. Maybe we should do a paper. Molly, let's. We could do a fantastic paper with what you've seen tonight."

"Third job offer I've had today."

"Third?"

"Yes, John wants to make me deputy, Dave wants to hire me as his bookkeeper, and you want a researcher."

"Best offer you've had all day, sounds like to me."

"No way. No, love, I'm just beginning to learn to talk like a native. I could never learn to talk like a sociologist."

"But it's easy," Ken protested. "You say anything you want to say; the only rule is all papers must end with the sentence 'More research is needed.' Sometimes you can say, 'Additional research is needed.' "

"Well, maybe you're right, maybe it is the best offer I've had all day, only I'm co-author, right, not just researcher?"

"Agreed." He laughed.

They finished the walk in silence, hugging each other against the predawn chill or against the ceaseless losses that mark the passing of human time. In the trees above them the cicadas thrummed, filling the dark with their ceaseless indifference.

ACKNOWLEDGMENTS

The Tricounty and all its institutions are fictional, but some very real people helped create them. Special thanks to Jenny Gilbert, a former grad student of mine; to Dave McBride, project supervisor for the Athens County Engineers office and amateur historian, for details on the roads and WIN towns in this region; and to Theresa Cline of our local Meals on Wheels program for details on operations and menus and her many insights into the culture of the elderly. I also want to thank a lot of people I can't name. The population is low in this region, so low that the only organized local sport is the potluck supper. I figured no one here would believe the usual "any resemblance is coincidence" disclaimer, so I did the opposite. I told all my friends I was putting everyone I knew in this novel, except that I would give them some say in the creative process. They could first choose whether to be a victim or a suspect, and second, whether to be good or evil. (Most everyone chose to be an evil suspect.) For my part, if we didn't discuss their "character," I wouldn't let myself be inspired by them. Trouble was, so many people came forward with great character ideas, I couldn't possibly put them in one book. So, to all those of you who are here, you know who you are, and thank you. To all of you who have talked to me and *aren't* here, thank you, and I promise to write other books. And to everyone else, everyone I haven't talked to, any resemblance between you and a character here is not only coincidence, you're someone else entirely.